OF WEREWOLVES AND CURSES

EMMA HAMM

For the real life prince in my life, who proves that fairytales really do exist

CHAPTER 1

"What a lovely day to contemplate murder," Arrow snuffled, then plopped down beside her. His tail wasn't wagging and his teeth were bared in an impressive snarl.

Freya looked up from the map on the table. "And who exactly are we murdering?"

He stared her dead in the eyes and replied, "The Goblin King."

That would be rather problematic considering the Goblin King was very dear to both of them. She sighed and looked back to the map of the kingdom on the center of the gold table. Her father was out there, somewhere. And no one had a clue where the werewolf had fled. Someone had to have heard something.

But she supposed right now wasn't the time to figure all that out. She needed to help her friend rather than try to figure out where a wayward werewolf would run off to.

Sighing, she put her hand over the Summer Court and turned her entire attention to the handsome dog. They were in the castle's observatory, a rather strange room with swaying planets over their head. The two of them stood in the only section that was safe from all the flying projectiles.

A star circled overhead, the bright bulb casting shadows of planets and the metal arms that moved them. Freya adjusted her lavender gown, flipping the skirts over the small stool behind her while taking a seat.

Crossing her arms over her chest, she asked, "Why are we contemplating killing the Goblin King?"

"Because he refuses to see reason about anything. I told him the werewolf might be in the Autumn Court, but he's not talking with the Thief right now. I told him moving your mother in the western wing would be smarter, the view is nicer. Of course he won't move your mother farther away from Esther." He huffed out another angry growl. "I told him to put honey in his tea because he needs something sweet in his life, and he tipped it over onto the table and left breakfast without a word."

Freya winced. The Goblin King's horrible mood may have been her fault, considering she'd rushed up to this room to pour over the map for whatever details she could find. It wasn't like the map changed. No one had even spelled it to show what she wanted. But her heart told her to stare until something revealed itself. Maybe that was foolish.

"Ah," she replied. "Well, that horrible mood was my doing. I told him I would have breakfast with him because he had something important to tell me, and I forgot until this moment."

Arrow narrowed his eyes on her. "Right. So you were the one who unleashed the most terrifying goblin on us because you wanted to look at the map again."

"Apparently." She winced again, then cleared her throat. "I'm sorry?"

"No. No need to be sorry." Arrow stood up and walked over to the nearest window. Slashes of bright golden light illuminated the dust particles that swirled through the air. He hopped up onto a podium underneath a pointy star and stood in the light. "You have doomed us all to a horrible meeting. I will blame you when this is over."

"Meeting?" she asked.

The doors to the observatory busted open and a whole group of strange people walked in. Lux with his rat face and thin tail waving behind him. Esther, who was turning more faerie by the day. Her hands had already started growing pads on her fingertips. Her newly saved mother walked between them, eyes already sharpened with the wit and intent to save her husband.

Last, the Goblin King. He wore a glower that should have burned everyone around him to the ground. He squared his shoulders with aggression and stomped toward the table without even looking at Freya.

Right. So they were arguing.

She sighed and attempted a smile at the others. "Hello. It's good to see all of you."

Esther, as usual, was unaware of the tension that had entered the room with her. She flounced to her stool at the table, yellow dress billowing around her like a cloud. It perfectly matched her lovely blonde hair. "Morning, Freya! We missed you at breakfast."

Everyone in the room fell silent, holding their breath and staring at the Goblin King. He bared his teeth in a snarl and parroted Esther. "Yes, Freya. We missed you at breakfast. Where were you, considering you promised you would actually eat with the lot of us?"

Her cheeks burned. "I was here. Looking at the map and preparing for this meeting."

"Were you now?" He sat on his own stool directly across from her. "And did you find anything new? Anything worth wasting all of our time?"

She narrowed her gaze. If he wanted to play this game, then she would keep up with him. He could be as passive aggressive as he wanted. Freya had grown up with a little sister and she knew how to ignore children when they were being annoying.

Pointing to a small mark near the Summer Court on the map, she replied, "Yes, I think this is worth considering. There were a few books in the library that claimed the Summer Court was a home of sorts for the werewolves before the fae killed them all off. I think it would be interesting to research this place."

"The Summer Court is not where he would go," Eldridge snarled. "The curse wouldn't let him. He would know how dangerous it was to go there."

"Are you so sure of that?" She stood and slapped her hands down on the table. "I think you don't want to agree with me this morning. You know that it's a perfectly acceptable place to look into, and the more places we research, the better. It's not like the Summer Court is that far away."

"I think you need to be better about remembering promises!" He stood as well, mirroring her position with his fingers a hair's breadth from hers. "I forgot how frustrating it was to have mortals around when you can all lie through your teeth."

"Are you calling me a liar because I forgot to have breakfast with you?" She leaned so close she could see the sparks flying in his eyes.

This was ridiculous. He couldn't claim she was a liar because she wasn't catering to his every whim. She had a life outside of him, no matter how much he didn't want her to.

Her mother cleared her throat, interrupting them. "I understand that you two may be a little frustrated with each other, but can we please focus on finding my husband before you tear each other's heads off?"

Eldridge snarled. "I don't want to rip her head off, I want a few moments of her time, which is apparently very precious these days."

"We sleep in the same bedroom," she gritted through her teeth. "If you had something to say, then you can say it when we're there."

"Our bedroom should be a place of happiness and rest. I refuse to talk about anything but joyous things within those walls."

"Ah ha!" She snapped her fingers and pointed in his face. "I knew you had something bad to tell me! Why would I want to hear even more bad news when that's all we've been talking about these days?"

He mirrored her action, pointing at her with a clawed finger. "You should want to talk to me about anything! That's what a team is. That's what people do in a relationship!"

Arrow hopped up on the table in between them and shook hard. Water went flying throughout the room, soaking both Freya and Eldridge. She backed away from the table with a shriek.

"What in the world, Arrow!" She wiped water off her face before glaring. "How did you even get wet?"

Ah. That would be her sister holding an empty bucket in her hands that Esther quickly tossed to the side.

Freya glared at both of them.

Eldridge wiped water off his fine suit and grumbled. "You two with your pranks. Why were you getting involved?"

Neither of them knew how to answer their king. They looked at each other, then back to the table, then back at each other.

With a heavy sigh, Astrid stepped forward and answered his question. "We all understand the two of you are tense. A new relationship on top of all your responsibilities is particularly stressful. No one could ever say otherwise. However, you are both letting your stress get in the way of many things these days. We need you to focus on the task at hand, which is finding out where the wolf might be hiding. Whatever tiff you're in can wait until after that."

Had they poured water over Arrow just to cool Freya and Eldridge off? That seemed rather overkill.

Frowning, Freya pointed back to the map in the center of the table. "I already know where Dad is. I told you, this is the summer home of the wolves and he would return to it. There's no way he's anywhere else."

"And you know the faerie realm so well," Eldridge scoffed. He leaned over the map and read the name of the mark she'd pointed at. "Actually..."

Freya let out a grunt as he rounded the table and pushed her aside.

"Move," Eldridge said after shoving her.

"I didn't really have a choice not to," she grumbled. Freya jostled back to her position in front of the map, hip checking him out of her way. "This is the spot I read about. You gave me the book on the werewolves, you know."

"Yes, I remember." His brows furrowed in concentration, he looked over the roads that were near the small town of Sunhold. "I remember this place from when I was a boy. It's near the Summer palace."

"I must have missed it on my travels throughout all the kingdoms," she snarled.

"Easy, now you sound like your father." He tapped his claw against the mark on the map and gave a quick nod. "I take back what I said. You were right, this is a good place to start."

Freya could have flipped the table; his words made her so angry. Of course it was the right spot. She was the only one who had dedicated every single day to researching the wolves and their history. She'd read countless books, at least twenty, recounting the wolves' movements, the battles, even the interviews the fae had conducted on the wolves they had captured.

Her mind was painted with bloody battles and horrible endings for people like her father. Sometimes it felt like she had lived through the moments with the wolves themselves, and that was difficult to think about. The stories had even slipped into her dreams until she was frightened to fall asleep.

In short, if anyone knew where the wolves were, it was Freya.

She balanced her hip on the side of the table and eyed him with a lifted brow. "And?"

"And what?"

"Are you going to apologize for automatically thinking I was wrong? I wasn't. I want to hear you say it." Maybe that was because she found it ridiculously attractive when he admitted she was right.

Eldridge snarled and bared his teeth.

Astrid rolled her eyes and held out an arm for the others, gesturing toward the door. "Come on, then. Now that we have a clue, we'll all research Sunhold. In the meantime, I suggest you two get your argument over with. Otherwise, you're going to annoy the rest of us. Come, children. Now."

Though she might have expected Lux and Esther to balk at being called children, everyone filed out of the room with surprising swiftness. They raced to the door and quietly closed it behind them, leaving Freya alone with a very angry Goblin King.

She shrugged, arms still hugged tightly over her chest. "What? What could you possibly need to tell me, Eldridge? You made us look ridiculous in front of them."

"Oh, I made us look ridiculous?" He pressed a hand over his heart. "That was me doing that? Not you?"

"Well, it couldn't be me. I can't look foolish, that's your job."

The growl that erupted from his chest would have put a werewolf to shame. Eldridge lunged for her, hands tunneling into her hair, and yanked her forward.

He kissed her with all the anger that he was feeling. Lips hard and unyielding, teeth nipping at her mouth, and tongue demanding to be let in. For all that she was mad at him, Freya was more than happy to let him take out his frustration like this.

She grabbed him by his waistband, tugging him closer to her with a grunt. "You make me so angry," she hissed against his lips.

"And you drive me mad," he growled. With a swift movement, he scooped his arm underneath her bottom and tossed her on top of the table. Map be damned, she would let him do whatever he wanted.

Eldridge returned his hand to the back of her neck, forcefully holding her in place and locking her lips to his. He ground himself against her hips. Every rolling movement sent her closer to the edge. He consumed her. Devoured her whole and she could think of nothing but him.

The Goblin King who wanted her even when he was angry. Even when he wanted to yell and scream and shout. Instead, he channeled all that energy into kissing her. Loving her. Turning her thoughts away from anger.

His hot breath echoed in her ear. His body moved with power and barely leashed rage. And she wouldn't have it any other way.

He made her entire body ache, tense, and release more times than she could count. He took magic from her body until it felt like all her energy was rolling off her in waves.

Finally, he stopped. She pressed her hands to his sweat slicked back and held on for dear life. Freya wanted just a few more moments when they were one, not two.

Eldridge leaned down and pressed his lips to her shoulder. "I should have apologized before we started all that."

"I think it was apology enough." Goodness, her voice was raspy. She finally released her hold on his muscles and leaned back. "I think we ruined the map, though."

He leaned to look at all the drops of sweat they'd left in the smudged ink. "Ah well." He shrugged. "I have more."

She moaned as he pulled away from her, leaving behind a sense of emptiness. "No. You know I hate it when you do that."

Eldridge tugged his pants up but grinned at her with far too much male pride. He leaned toward her again and tugged her in for another hard kiss. "I know, darling, but we both have to start our day."

Oh, if only he wasn't right. They had a lot to do, and not enough time for either of them to do everything.

Sighing, she hopped down from the table and tugged her dress back into place. Her hair, however, she could do nothing to save. "I suppose you're right. And you know how much I hate it when you're right."

"As always." He pulled his pale shirt back over his head. "But a king has many responsibilities."

"Mm." Running her fingers through the tangled mass of her hair, Freya paused and looked at him. "What did you have to say, anyway?"

A small flicker in his eyes gave away that he wasn't telling her the entire truth. Or that he was spinning words when he replied, "It's not important anymore. I'll tell you later, my love."

He silenced her with another kiss before walking away, whistling as he went.

Freya wondered if he'd ever tell her. Obviously he had something on his mind that was important enough to put him in a foul mood. And she wouldn't always be around to entertain him on a table.

Although it had been entertaining.

No, she had to stop thinking like that. After all, there was a job to be done.

A king had to be a king, he was right. But a hero also had to save. She needed to find her mother and the others so they could figure out the next steps in finding her father.

Sunhold. Perhaps another adventure awaited them already.

CHAPTER 2

Freya found her family in the library with their noses stuck in books. That was... odd. Her family rarely wanted to read about the lands they needed to go to. They were action people, not readers.

She leaned against the door frame and watched them with a careful eye until Esther looked up and yawned.

"Oh, Freya," she said. "We wondered when you would finish with your argument. Did you tell the Goblin King to stuff it?"

Lux snickered and pressed his hand to his mouth.

Oh, they were all children. Rolling her eyes, she walked into the library and sat down in the empty chair. "You were all listening at the door, weren't you? That's disgusting."

"You're telling me," Arrow grumbled from his seat on a pile of blankets next to the window. He turned the page of his open book. The worn red leather gleamed in the sunlight. "I could have gone my entire life without hearing what I did. The others might be able to run and not remember it, but it took forever for me to get far enough."

"That's gross." Her cheeks burned so hot, she thought she might burst into flames. "You shouldn't be listening at doors. You got what you deserved."

He shuddered. "Nightmares. Nightmares for life."

Lux finally couldn't hold his laughter in anymore. He set his book on his lap, the book Freya now realized was upside down, and tilted his head back with roaring laughter. He didn't even try to hold in the mirth that shook through his shoulders and entire form. The rest of the room dissolved into laughter as well.

Her mother was clearly trying to pull herself back together, and Astrid held up her hand for them all to stop screaming. "All right, everyone. That's enough teasing. I, for one, am glad that the Goblin King and his hero have given up being angry with each other. It makes everything else so much easier."

"Thank you, Mother," she said.

It was the first time she'd said words like that since she had gotten her mother back. They felt odd to say, but somehow right at the same time. Maybe someday it would get easier to talk to the woman who had birthed her. Maybe. She hoped.

Clearing her throat, she pointed to the book Arrow was actually reading. "I'm guessing that's the only book in this room that will give us more information about where Dad is?"

Arrow looked up from the pages, obviously bored with them all. "You are correct. No one else is working but me."

"Right." She bit her lip. "I suppose that makes sense considering everyone else was more enamored with gossip. What have you found?"

He stood up and shook himself, then pinched the book between both paws and walked it over to her. "Sunhold was the summer home for most werewolves, as you said. However, I think there are a few distinctions that you should know about. Namely that the wolves chose to go here. They weren't called like turtles to their birthplace. He might have gone somewhere else because he knows how dangerous this place is for his kind."

Astrid straightened in her chair, her amused expression changing to one of severe worry. "I wouldn't discount that, but I think it's unlikely he'd think that far ahead. Your father knew little about the werewolves. He stayed with us because he could.

Leaving them was an easy choice for him, so he wouldn't know their history."

A low hum vibrated in Freya's throat as she thought about those words. "You said Dad was bitten when we were young?"

"Yes."

"How young?" She gestured to the red leather book in Arrow's paws. "This claims the wolves were all killed off. And where was he when he was bitten? That... It doesn't make a lot of sense, is all."

Astrid shook her head, brows furrowed. "I don't know the answer to that. Your father said he had to go home. He never told me which court his family was from, and I never met them. He might have come from the Summer Court, and maybe that's why he went there? If the wolves were even there to bite him. You said there weren't many left."

Wincing, Freya shook her head with disappointment. "There are too many holes. We would only be able to guess that he might be here."

"I can send some messengers and see if they find anything," Arrow said. He patted the book and placed it in her lap. "This might help with understanding the wolves better, if you haven't read it yet. But I think we all need to understand that he isn't in his right mind. He's not your father at the moment."

She remembered reading that. Freya looked down at the book and wished it would reveal further secrets to her.

Esther asked, "What does Arrow mean? Not in his right mind?"

"He wasn't killing pixies only because he wanted to help Mom," Freya replied. "The wolves have three forms. Human. Wolf. And then that twisted being we saw in the Spring Court. He doesn't know what he's doing, and he doesn't understand us when we're talking to him. Maybe a little, but they aren't... Well, they aren't human when they're like that."

Arrow coughed. "It's a cursed form, Miss Esther. Painful to be in and even worse on the mind. Your father probably doesn't remember who he even is. He just knew that the human inside him was tied to your mother, and he couldn't leave her side for that reason."

She hated seeing her sister's expression twist to sadness. Esther wanted everyone to be happy and together. She wasn't built for a life like this, with their family fractured into pieces.

Freya could only hope that they got him back quickly. She also wouldn't mind having them all back together again. It might be nice to have a family unit in the faerie realm.

The book in her lap held some answers she searched for, and that was a start. Freya palmed it and stood up again. "All of you keep looking for anything that might help in the long run. Nothing is too vague for us to take seriously. I hope you understand the urgency of this."

Lux saluted her. "You've got it, Queen Killer."

She pointed at him with a frown. "Don't call me that."

"Sorry, it's the name you've been given." He reclined in his chair, hands linked behind his head and ankles crossed over each other. "You can't undo a nickname once it's given to you."

"Watch me."

Freya left the library, battling hope with every step. She knew better than to let herself get excited about the opportunity this might provide. Her father could be exactly where she had pinned him down to be.

Sunhold. The town that the fae had abandoned all those years ago and then taken over by werewolves. It was the perfect place for them to enjoy the heat for a little while. She knew why their kind would want to stay there.

But now she had to face the Summer Lord again. She wasn't looking forward to going back to the Summer Court and seeing all those masked elves. They had made her intensely uncomfortable.

Freya didn't know where she was going, only that she had to go somewhere. She found herself back at the room she shared with Eldridge.

Her heart knew who she wanted to talk to. The only man who had ever understood the wild need in her heart to be more than what she was. The only man who had given her permission to be herself. Even when she was being hard headed.

Freya nudged the door open and found Eldridge waiting for her. He stood in front of the floor to ceiling window, hands held behind his back. A galaxy swirled in front of him, the stars glowing brightly and then disappearing as they faded from life.

She didn't know how she always found him so easily in this palace. The hallways were difficult to maneuver, and Eldridge never told her where he was going. But no matter how challenging it should have been, if she wanted to find him, then she could.

"Ah," he said as she closed the door behind her. "That didn't take long."

"Well, they weren't working all that hard." She waved the red leather book in the air. "Arrow was the only one to find anything, and it's not exactly helpful."

"How so?"

She sighed and tossed the book onto the bed. "It's mostly about how the werewolf mind thinks, and the history of why they went to Sunhold. I'm sure I've read it already, but I've read so many of them all the words blend together."

He turned around, and she was enraptured with the sight of him all over again. Those broad shoulders had filled out after his torture in the Winter Court. His glossy dark hair fell over his shoulder and those pointed teeth gleamed in the dim light of the stars. His silver skin reflected the light as though he really were made of metal, and every fiber of her soul wanted to jump on him again.

It had been like that ever since they returned to his kingdom, though. They couldn't keep their hands off each other. Even when they tried.

She shook her head to dispel the hungry thoughts from her mind. She needed to focus, not lust after the Goblin King. "I still think Sunhold is our best bet. My mother doesn't think he would avoid the location because he knows next to nothing about werewolves."

The bright heat of passion faded from Eldridge's eyes. "Are you so sure about that?"

"Why would he know anything? He'd grown up here, yes, but the fae don't consort with werewolves. You said so yourself." She tilted her head to the side. "Or do they?"

"It depends on who his family was." He released his hands and raised them in a gesture of disbelief. "I know there are a few fae out there who have surprised you, my dear. Some of us aren't as... hateful as others. If they thought the werewolves were useful to whatever cause they had, then it is likely someone might have taken a few of them in."

She narrowed her eyes. "That sounds like an Autumn Court choice to me."

"What would make you think a goblin would be interested in a wolf?" He scoffed, but she saw the nervous glint in his eyes. "None of us would take a werewolf under our wing."

"Look at Arrow." The more she thought about it, the more it made sense. "He looks like a dog. Logic would bring me to believe there are more goblins who look like wolves than dogs. It's not impossible to think that someone who looks like them may have been interested in helping someone who shares the same features."

"It's a start to finding your lineage." The Goblin King looked disturbed.

Freya couldn't stand that expression. "What? What are you thinking?"

He pressed a hand to his mouth but didn't hide his smile fast enough. "I hope we don't find out that we're related."

"Eldridge!" All the blood drained from her face. "Please tell me you don't believe there's a chance of that."

He burst out laughing. But that still didn't make her feel any better. Could they really be related? She was already turning green at the thought. She couldn't let him go. He was everything to her now, even if she wasn't very good at telling him that yet.

But related?

Eldridge reached for her and tugged her into his arms. "No, my love. We can't be related."

"But if you're from the Autumn Court, and I'm from the Autumn Court, then how can you be so sure?" she asked, her mouth mashed against his chest.

"Because otherwise I would have heard of your father. There is no one in my family who went missing, and we did not partake in any changeling swaps of children." He leaned back and brushed his hands over her head, smoothing her hair back from her face. "And my darling, your father grew up here, but that doesn't make him related to any of us. Changelings are different, remember?"

Right. Even though she could perform magic, her father wasn't fae. They didn't know how all that would have affected his children, but he still wasn't a faerie.

Thank goodness.

Blowing out a long breath of relief, she nodded. "All right. Well, don't scare me like that next time."

"Why not?" he arched a brow. "I've heard there are quite a few mortals who like keeping everything in the same bloodline. We'd create a noble family lineage no one could deny."

Freya pulled herself out of his arms and slapped him on the shoulder. "Stop it. It's not funny."

"It is a little." He held up fingers and pinched them together. "Just a tiny amount, maybe?"

"Not at all," she scolded. But she couldn't stop the grin from spreading across her face. "Fine. Maybe a little. But can we focus, my Goblin King? What are we doing now?"

He rolled his eyes and backed her toward the bed. "First, I'm going to enjoy an afternoon with my dear hero that I used to dream about when I was a boy. And then we're going to start packing for a trip to Sunhold."

"Another trip? So soon?" She veered away from the bed. "I should probably start packing now, then."

"Oh no, you don't." He caught her around the waist and tumbled with her onto the mattress.

They didn't start packing until very late that night.

CHAPTER 3

Eldridge opted for horses this time, and Arrow was less than happy about it. He grumbled from the back of Freya's horse about how horrible the travel conditions were. He was more a cart kind of goblin. Or at the very least, a goblin who would ride in a carriage.

Not a horse.

Never a horse.

If she had to listen to him complain any more, she would explode. The goblin seriously underestimated how much patience she would have during this trip. If he said one more thing, she was going to dump him off the saddle and ride off into the sunset. He could walk to the Summer Court.

Eldridge kicked his horse until they were walking side by side. "Arrow, you can always walk if this is such a great inconvenience."

The goblin dog snapped his jaw shut and glared at the Goblin King. "You know I can't keep up."

"No, I wouldn't imagine you could. But I'd give you a map."

Arrow grumbled and settled back down on the pack he was holding onto for dear life. Freya couldn't say she was the biggest fan of the horses, either. They weren't normal creatures like she was used to in the mortal realm. These horses were larger, nearly two men tall and wide enough that she had to sit side saddle.

She glanced over at Eldridge, who looked too pleased with himself.

"You know," she started. "We didn't have to take the horses."

"Of course not, but I enjoy riding them." He patted his own horse on the neck. "Don't you?"

She wasn't going to answer that. He already knew what she was going to say, considering the bright glint in his eyes.

The horses weren't all that bad, but their travel was now uncomfortable and she also would have preferred the carriage. Though, they had lovely fresh air to breathe on this journey, rather than a stuffy box with all three of them packed inside.

"Fine," she admitted. "This is a lovely way to travel and I do feel better for having all this air around us."

"I thought you might."

Arrow snarled from behind them, but didn't chime in with his opinion. They both knew what it would be, anyway.

She let them travel in silence for a few more moments. Tilting her head back, she let her horse walk as he wished and enjoyed the sun on her face. A slight breeze toyed with her hair, tangling in the long strands and brushing them off her shoulders. Every step brought them farther from the chill of autumn and into the heat of the Summer Court.

"You know," she said, starting the conversation that they needed to have, even though she didn't know if he would tell her the truth. "When I was first in the Summer Court, it appeared that you knew the Summer Lord well."

"Did I?" Eldridge asked, playing dumb to her question. "I don't know why you'd think that."

"Well, because you were sitting on matching thrones, for a start. But also because there were a few jabs that each of you flung at each other that were more brotherly than they were noble." She frowned, trying to remember the exact words.

Strangely, she couldn't. There were so many moments between

the Summer Court and now that she honestly remembered little other than the highlights of that journey. The elves without faces. The beautiful castle with all its seashell glory. She even remembered the Summer Lord himself, wearing his pressed white suit and the gleam of his skin like a rare pearl. Even the labyrinth where the Goblin King had tried to trick her into getting lost.

But that was it. She didn't remember what was said or even how she had gotten there.

Eldridge shrugged and then relented to her questioning. "The Summer Lord and I were childhood friends. Both young noblemen who had no right to be nobles at the time. We were wild and perhaps a little too... aggressive with our tactics in learning how to be men. We were friends for a very long time and then had a falling out."

Oh, she had so many questions. Freya shielded her eyes from the sun so she could look at him with a little more focus. "You were friends? And aggressive tactics? What on earth are you talking about?"

Arrow poked his head around her shoulder, resting his chin against her arm. "He means they were idiots back in the day. My father used to tell me about those foolish things they did when they were young. Both of them were trying to prove themselves worthy of a throne so they went off gallivanting around the countryside trying to bring back the most impressive kill. Or woo the most beautiful lady."

Eldridge was quick to interrupt his friend. "We never did any of that. Most of the court thought we both were unfit for a throne and ignored us. We were just children trying to prove ourselves."

"What kind of kills did you think you were going to bring back?" she asked. Freya tried very hard not to focus on the latter because that would only make her frustrated and jealous.

"Mostly the heads of fabled beasts. A few stag were known to glow in the dark, their hides were so white. And there were a couple..." He paused, then sighed. "Werewolves back in the day. They were menaces to all faeries, and we wanted to take care of that issue for our people."

"Ah." So that was why he hadn't wanted to tell her. "You were worried I wouldn't like that you hunted the wolves. I assumed you did, Eldridge. You've been around much longer than my father has been alive."

"Perhaps." He shifted on his horse, gripping the reins too tight. "But that doesn't make me any less ashamed of my actions. Even back then, I knew it was wrong to hunt them."

As much as Freya wanted to say he was right, she wasn't so sure. What she had read in those books made her think the fae had no choice in the matter. The wolves, like her father had proven, were too strong. They hunted the poor faeries down and pulled them apart. Rarely did they eat their prey, they simply wanted to feel flesh beneath their claws.

But his brows were furrowed, and she knew he was already slipping into those dark memories that made him feel like a monster. She couldn't let him linger there. Not in the war, not with the death of the wolves that were now too close to her father. He didn't deserve that.

She changed the subject to something she really didn't want to talk about. "And the ladies?"

Arrow ducked back to his spot on the horse.

At the same time, Eldridge turned to look at her with a shocked expression. "The who?"

"The ladies you were attempting to woo. The most beautiful women in the court, I assume. Who were they?" She looked straight ahead and tried not to give away the anger riding her shoulders. "I can't imagine what the lovely women of the faerie courts must look like."

"Oh, they far surpass any creatures you may have seen in your life. Their skin is made of moonlight, some of them of darkness. Their hair is spun sun rays and their eyes are chips of gemstones.

No one is more lovely than the ladies of the faerie courts." He sighed dramatically.

She wanted to hit him. Freya knew that this would be the answer, of course, but it still stung. She would never be one of those faeries made of the elements and most beautiful places in the realms.

Eldridge chuckled.

"What?" she asked, refusing to look at him still.

"Freya."

"What do you want, Eldridge?"

He snapped his clawed fingers in front of her face, forcing her to look at the laughter dancing in his eyes. "None are as lovely as you, my dear. I would never be so foolish as to compare you to the fickle and far off fae. Not a single one captured my attention as you have, and none ever will again."

If she blushed any harder, Freya would set her horse on fire. It was so easy to get caught up in those jealous thoughts that she would never be enough compared to the faeries he'd been with before. But she also knew the reality of their story.

He had chosen her. Not one of them. And Eldridge could have chosen one of the fae at any point. Every single day he reminded her that he had and would continue to choose her. She needed to remember that a little more.

Sighing, she tucked a strand of hair behind her ear and nodded. "Right. Well, I suppose the only other thing I want to know is why you and the Summer Lord are no longer friends. And don't try to get around it by saying you lived different lives and drifted away from each other. I saw you two together, and there were no remnants of fond memories."

Eldridge stiffened. He gripped the reins a little too tightly again, uncomfortable with this question. "The Summer Lord and I had a difference in opinion."

Freya waited for him to continue, but he didn't. He let the conversation end there and would have kept on with their journey without ever explaining himself.

She huffed out an angry breath. "Well? What was the difference in opinion?"

"Do you really need to know?"

"What if it's important? Yes, I need to know!"

Eldridge threw the reins down and tossed his hands up into the air. "I didn't think he should become the Summer Lord. I thought it was too much pressure for him, and I didn't see his ability to be a good leader. And when I told him that, he threw me out of his court and vowed I'd never set foot in it again."

She could understand how that would be hurtful, especially from someone who the Summer Lord had thought was a very close friend. "But obviously you did visit the court again."

"I did." His eyes narrowed on the road ahead of them. "When I surpassed them all and became the Goblin King."

Ah, and she supposed that was also a pain point between the two of them. They had both wanted a throne, although Eldridge had only wanted to be the Autumn Thief. And he had been for a time, before it was revealed just how truly powerful he really was.

She could only imagine that stung when the Summer Lord had wanted to prove himself alongside his friend, who was no longer his friend at all.

Sighing, she kept her eyes on the road as well. "I hope that won't sting in his mind for too much longer. After all, he has a court just like you."

"And I rule over him. The friend who betrayed him when he needed me most."

Right. That didn't bode well for the end of their journey.

Freya waited until she saw the Summer Castle appear on the horizon. It was beautiful with its abalone shell walls and the whirling towers that rose like pointed seashells. White sand spread out around the base of it and the gardens were lush, deep emerald that spread around the entire land like everything could grow in this soil.

Elves dotted the distance. They wandered through the

gardens and pet the plants as they went. They lived in a jungle of greenery and blue skies.

She had the strangest thought: that no one here had ever experienced hardship. They had never gone hungry and they likely never would. If only they could understand what it felt like to have their stomach crawling with hunger, then they might understand humans a little better.

Maybe they would all get their faces if they did that.

"Here we are," Eldridge said. "I hope you're ready for what we're about to do."

"I suppose I am. I haven't ever been to a court I couldn't handle yet." Freya straightened her posture, hoping she looked intimidating and prepared for this moment. "Are you ready?"

"I'm never ready for a trip to the Summer Court." His haunted expression darkened as they got even closer to the castle. "I know he'll help us. He's never been able to stop himself from being called to the hunt. I'm just not certain where he'll go from there. He's unpredictable at best. Always be on your guard."

She remembered. The Summer Lord had made an impression when she first met him, and not in a good way. The man had been mostly disappointing. Freya would never forget the acrid scent of alcohol on his breath, or how she had gotten him so drunk that a mere mortal had stolen from him. It wasn't impressive.

It was downright sad.

One of the elves caught sight of them and ran into the castle. She knew this was the moment when they had to look their best. Freya squared her shoulders, smoothed her pale blue riding outfit into place, and kept her eyes straight ahead. She didn't look at any of the elves, because she didn't want them to see the fear behind her visage of bravery.

The doors to the castle opened as they rode up to the front gates. The Summer Lord looked exactly as she remembered him.

He wore a gold suit this time, and Freya knew it wasn't meant to be mistaken for yellow. He glowed like some kind of Sun god. The fabric appeared to be stitched with actual metal because the collar was stiff as he walked down the steps and approached them. His dark skin was glorious, oiled to perfection and highlighting the vivid darkness of his eyes. The entire sea was contained in the depths of his eyes. But not a kind sea.

"Welcome back to the Summer Court," he called out, opening his arms wide even as his eyes narrowed on them. "To what do I owe the absolute pleasure of the Goblin King and the Queen Killer's presence?"

If Eldridge replied, she feared they would lose all chances of getting the Summer Lord to help them. Freya cleared her throat and answered for him. "We're looking for my father, and considering the tale is one of intrigue and magic, we thought you may like to help."

"Your father?" He tilted his head to the side and pursed his lips. "I don't think I'm very interested in hearing that story. Mortals are so tiresome."

"He's a changeling," Freya replied. She knew that word alone would capture his attention, but she had no fear of saying who her father really was. "And then he was bitten by a werewolf when I was young."

The Summer Lord's eyes lit up with a burning passion. "Did you say werewolf?"

She nodded. "I did."

He looked at the Goblin King, then back to her. With a sigh, the Summer Lord gestured for them to get off their horses. "Fine, then. I'll suffer the Goblin King in my court for a little while. I'm curious to know more about your werewolf father and why you think he might be here."

Well, it was a start. Freya made eye contact with Eldridge and shrugged. At least they'd gotten the Summer Lord's attention for the time being.

CHAPTER 4

T hey trailed the Summer Lord into the Summer Castle, past the giant stairwell overrun with flowers. Freya stared up at the mosaic on the ceiling as they passed, and she remembered the fear she'd felt the first time she was here. Sneaking through the palace and hoping that no one would find her.

The elves were terrifying to her then. Their masks didn't cover enough of their smooth faces. And she so greatly feared what they would do if they found her.

Of course, none of them had. It had been the Goblin King to find her in that strange room with its single stairwell leading to nowhere. How could she ever forget his fingers trailing up her spine? It was the first time they'd ever touched skin to skin.

A tremble shook through her shoulders. Without even looking at her, Eldridge put his hand on her back and mimicked the movement he had used when he helped tighten the corset. Almost as though he knew what she was thinking about.

He distracted her the entire time it took them to get to the small office. The warm colors of blues and golds caught her attention, but she couldn't stop thinking about Eldridge's hand. He smoothed his thumb at her waist and she couldn't focus. Not on the Summer Lord. Not on what they had to do. All she could think about was him and his damned fingers.

Eldridge had to tell the entire story to the Summer Lord. And when he was finished, they were dismissed to a private room until the Lord decided whether or not he wanted to help them.

She was just pleased to get out of everyone's eye. She was going to combust if they didn't give her a little privacy with the man she loved.

The man she loved whom she hadn't told yet. But someday soon she would say it. She would tell him how much she loved him and just how much he meant to her happiness.

When they finally got into the room that looked like the inside of a clamshell, Arrow snarled. "I'll be back. You two obviously need some time with each other and I can't stand it any longer. You were much more fun when you weren't..." He gestured up and down with a paw. "This."

The dog left the room and then she was alone with Eldridge again. She stared up at him, silhouetted by the bright sun through the glass doors that led out onto their private balcony. It wasn't fair that he looked so good. Like he was still put together while she was falling apart.

"Were you distracting me on purpose?" she asked, her voice wavering.

"Maybe. I enjoyed your reactions." The expression on his face was far too smug. "Besides, I know the story as well as you do. I could tell it while you were trying to hold yourself together."

Freya stomped her foot in frustration. "How dare you? I should have been the one to inform him about my father!"

"You were preoccupied with your thoughts." He shrugged and reached for her like he was going to tug her into his arms. "And I find that I quite like you when you're distracted. You're adorable when your cheeks are that red, you know that, don't you?"

She slapped his hand. "What did you even say? And did you cast some kind of spell on me or something? I don't remember any of it."

And that was terrifying. Freya didn't know why those memories or thoughts were gone, but they absolutely were. She couldn't remember a single thing Eldridge had said, only that he was talking about her father and slowly tracing the bumps of her spine the entire time.

"I told him all he needs to know, and that was it. You can tell him more later if you want." Eldridge walked over to the bed and laid down, lifting his arms over his head as pillows. "But I thought maybe you would want a diversion in the meantime."

"I think I've been distracted enough for one day, thank you very much." Although, he was very tempting all laid out like that. She wanted to lick him from his knees all the way to the top of his head, but they didn't have time. "How did the Summer Lord respond, though? Does he have any idea where my father might be?"

Eldridge sighed and scrubbed a hand over his face. "No, Freya. No one knows where he might be, but that's all right. We know the greatest likelihood is that he's here, isn't it?"

She supposed. But that wasn't quite good enough for her. Not when there was an opportunity here to meet with the Summer Lord and find out so much more information than they already knew. If the werewolves used to live here, then surely the Summer Lord had texts that were filled with more knowledge.

"Are you going to sleep the day away?" she asked. "What about finding the Summer Lord's library? We could at least see if he has any more volumes that might give us a few more clues."

"You can try to leave if you want. He made it very clear that we weren't wandering about his castle when he didn't trust us." Eldridge gestured toward the door. "Go ahead, though. Be my guest."

Ominous. Freya strode to the door, opened it, and nearly bumped into the back of the giant elf who stood on the other side of the door. He turned back to stare at her, his mask covered in the scales of a lizard. His eyes were blank from emotion and the terrifying mask was enough to send her back into the room with a swift slam of the door.

"Right," she muttered. "Apparently I won't be going to that library after all. But really, what is a room full of books going to do? It's not dangerous for me to be in there."

She turned around, wondering whether there was another exit, only to find that Eldridge had disappeared. There wasn't even an indent on the bed where he had been lying.

And had the room changed? The walls weren't quite right. At least, not like she remembered. Perhaps it was the sheen of color that was different.

The most glaring change, however, was the balcony itself. No longer were the windows looking out toward the sea, but into another room. The seashell quality of the walls changed to a shimmering green, and she didn't think it was a bathing area.

"Eldridge?" she whispered. The magic inside her stretched, seeking him out because she feared losing him forever if she didn't. "I need you here with me, now. I think something in this room is trying to hide you from me."

She felt him trying to find her. His magic was just so far away from her that it was hard to latch onto. But he'd taught her how to find him. No matter the cost to each other.

And in this strange, shimmering room, Freya feared she was in a lot more danger than she realized.

She reached out in her mind's eye and tugged hard. She pulled him through whatever barrier stood between them and felt him doing the same. Together, hand over hand, they fought to be beside one another again.

Finally, she saw the faint outline of his shadowy form. Freya held out her hand and felt him touch her fingers. With one final heave of energy and power, she pulled him through the veil and into the room she'd been transported to.

Eldridge was breathing hard, sweat slicking his brow. "What was that?" he snarled.

"I have no idea. One moment I was in our room, then I closed the door and suddenly, I wasn't there anymore." Freya turned fearful eyes toward the balcony that should have been looking out to see. "And the room changed. Quite a bit, actually."

He followed her gaze and blew out a long breath. "That's not supposed to happen."

"I can't imagine magic is ever supposed to happen. But what do you think it is?" Freya touched a hand to his shoulder. "Did the Summer Lord curse us?"

"No," he replied. Then he shook his head and cleared his throat as if he were trying to pull out of a memory. "I mean, I don't know if he cursed us. He might have. But the forest, Freya. That's what is not supposed to happen. The forest is part of the Summer Lord's magic. It's an advisor, of sorts. And it isn't supposed to appear for anyone but the Summer Lord himself."

"Oh." She looked to the trees and fear made her heart race again. "That doesn't sound good."

"It isn't." He took a step toward the balcony, only to be shoved back by the same magic that had tried to hide from him. "I don't know why it's fighting me. I'm the Goblin King. I'm here to help the forest and those it serves. I don't..."

Freya understood.

It was plain and simple. The forest didn't want to speak to the Goblin King. No one could argue the truth of that fact as the forest shoved him back yet again. The trees wanted to speak with someone. They had a story to tell, but it was not the Goblin King who should hear it.

"I think it wants to speak to me," she whispered.

A sudden wind caught her words and echoed them back through the air. But this time, the sounds were warped. "Speak to her," it whispered.

Eldridge looked at her, then the balcony, then shook his

head. "No. You can't go in there alone. I've never even been inside that forest, and I have no idea what might wait for you through those doors. It's too dangerous."

"As dangerous as fighting the Goblin King? Or killing the Winter Princess? Perhaps as dangerous as finding out the Spring Maiden was lying?" Freya approached the doors, completely unhindered by the magic. She gave Eldridge a sad smile. "Or maybe you meant it's more dangerous than seeking out a werewolf."

"Freya." He reached out his hand for her, struggling to lift it as the magic shoved him again. "I'm begging you not to do this without me."

She looked back to the room beyond the balcony that turned more green as she watched. Leaves broke through the seashell texture of the walls, and she could almost hear a voice calling out to her. It wanted to speak, and she didn't think denying the forest what it wanted was all that smart. In fact, she'd argue it was rather foolish to deny the trees anything. After all, they'd been here a lot longer than either Freya or Eldridge.

"I don't have a choice," she whispered.

She gave him one last look, just in case it was the last time she saw him. She could see how much this was killing him.

"Freya," he growled one last time. "There's too much left unsaid between us. Let me come with you. We can fight against this magic if we're together."

She felt the power of that forest pressing against her back. It was shoving her toward the doors, pulling at her very soul until she felt it slip underneath her tongue and waggle the appendage for her. "I don't want to fight it," she whispered. "I want to hear what it has to say."

"Freya!"

His shout echoed in her ears, but she couldn't stop herself. Freya reached for the handles of the balcony doors and pulled them open. They were light in her grasp, oiled perfectly so there wasn't a sound at all other than the Goblin King's shouting.

And then the doors were open and she couldn't hear him anymore. All she could hear was the sweet song of birds in the distance. The calm sound of wind rushing through leaves. Golden light spilled through an emerald canopy, and the whispers of the trees could barely be heard.

"She's coming," they said. "She has to take one more step and then she'll be here. Hush. Don't say too much. Not yet, he might still hear us."

These ancient beings desired to speak with a girl from the mortal realm. Such an honor couldn't be ignored. Freya looked behind her at the chaos in that in-between place.

Eldridge fought against the magic with everything he had. Shadows coiled around his fists and undulated like waves behind him. Lifting a hand, he pounded on the invisible barrier that stood between them.

If she gave him enough time, she knew he would shatter the forest's magic.

The Goblin King was a powerful man. He wielded magic with an iron fist.

She couldn't give him that choice. Freya took one more step, felt moss squish beneath her feet, and closed the doors firmly behind her.

CHAPTER 5

CHAPTER 5

The trees heaved a sigh of relief when it was just Freya and them. They waved their leaves in the wind, and all was calm. Their magic fell away from her shoulders and apparently she was free to wander wherever she wished to wander.

Freya hadn't been in the woods for what felt like years. The Spring Court was full of gardens and the deep depths of the mines. The Winter Court was all icy tundras and forgotten ice caves. And of course, Eldridge's kingdom was a galaxy of possibilities, but no trees.

And heavens, she had missed the trees.

Freya walked past their thick trunks with roots stretching deep into the ground. A knot inside of her untangled. Almost as though she recognized the forest she was in. As if she'd been here before.

She stepped over a fallen tree limb and froze when she saw two initials carved into the base of the nearest tree. She reached out and ghosted her fingertips over the carefully scratched letters. F and E.

Maybe she had been here before then.

"You've been in my life for longer than I realized, haven't you?" she asked quietly.

The tree bent into her touch, the bark shifting and moving. She thought she would have remembered a forest like this. But if this one had been leaking into the mortal realm, then maybe she wouldn't have known. They'd lived so close to a faerie portal, after all. It wasn't such a stretch to think that there might have been more that surrounded their home.

"My father used to live here, didn't he?" Her voice floated through the forest and tangled with the birdsong.

Freya didn't really think the trees would reply to her. They had more important things to do than listen to the mortal girl asking questions. And they had asked her here for a reason. They wouldn't care about her desire to find her father, and yet, she had hoped this journey would be the first step closer to him.

Rather than give up, she continued wandering underneath the giant branches, talking as she went.

"My father came here as a changeling child a long time ago." Freya carefully brushed a branch away from her face. "He loved the forest near our small cabin in the mortal realm. He said the world was empty without the scent of leaves on the ground and the wind rustling through the forest. If he didn't have that, then he surely would have wasted away."

The rattling branches over her head moved a little faster. As if they wanted her to keep telling them the story about her father. And if that's what they wanted, then Freya was all too happy to oblige.

She stepped over another log and felt her feet sink down into the ankle thick moss. "He used to call the forest the place where souls went to heal. Did you know that?"

The tree nearest to her rattled its branches ever louder. She'd take that as a yes.

"I'm looking for him," she admitted. "He lost himself for a bit, but I think he'd like to find his way back home. To me. To my mother and sister. Family was everything to him. At least, it was when I knew him."

Freya heard the deep hum of magic long before the trees shifted. She stopped and held out her arms as the world seemed to stretch and pull. The trees reordered themselves, first backing away from her and then snapping back into place. She blinked, and they were in a different spot than before.

The trees now created a row for her to walk down. The path was devoid of moss or greenery. And golden light speared through the suddenly much taller trees. The path led to a silver gate at the very end, with twisting coils silhouetted against the bright light.

"Ah," she mumbled. "I'm going to assume that is where you want me to go?"

That deep sound echoed through the forest again. It was a rumble of earth and loam. The voice of the land she walked upon.

She wasn't sure why she was listening to its whims. This was part of the faerie realm, and obviously this place could be leading her into a trap. Eldridge had thought that was what it was.

But this place felt like home. She'd been here before. She'd walked through these moss covered glens and she knew deep in her heart that this place would never try to harm her. It wanted to help.

She reached the gate and eased it open. It squealed loudly. Rust turned the hinges bright green, and moss grew up the edges. When was the last time someone had been here?

If this forest was supposed to be only visible to the Summer Lord, then she would have expected to see some movement. Wasn't it his duty to speak with the forest? Or was this merely an advisor who had remained silent for all these years?

She stepped into the hidden glade in the center of the forest. A small cage sat in the corner, made of roots and tangled vines that hung down from the branches of an impressively large tree. This great oak was covered in moss and lacked any leaves. But

Freya could still feel the strength that emanated from the beautiful, ancient being. It was still alive.

Movement behind the earthen cage caught her attention. At first, she thought it was nothing more than a squirrel or some other woodland creature. Then, the dark fur brushed up against the tangled roots and she recognized the color.

"Dad?" she whispered.

The movement within the cage stopped, and then a red eyed gaze turned toward her.

Freya lunged forward, reaching out her hand but not knowing if she should stick her fingers through the wooden bars. What if he didn't recognize her? The wolf could take off her fingers and those red eyes didn't seem to know who she was.

Her father continued his pacing. She peered through the shadows to see a sort of cave created deep in the hollow of the tree. This was more than just a cage, it was a prison meant to keep others out. Or something in.

"You're alive," she said, her voice breathy with relief. "I didn't think we'd find you so easily. But I'm so glad to see that you're alive."

Another voice interrupted her, and it was the strangest sound she'd ever heard. Like someone was taking their dying breath and speaking the words with lungs overfilled with air. "He's alive, but barely."

Cold chills rose up her arms. All her hairs lifted in fear and Freya had to talk herself into turning around. Whatever stood behind her was bound to be a terrifying monster, of sorts. She hoped it wasn't what she feared most. Some kind of spider or mashup of woodland animals that lived in the shadows.

Her imagination really was getting the best of her these days.

She stood and put her back to the cage, keeping far enough away that her father wouldn't be able to nip at her through the bars. At first, she didn't see the speaker at all. There was nothing behind her but trees covered in moss.

But then she realized that the voice had come from much

closer to her. The tree was the one that had spoken, but not quite the tree itself.

She looked to her right and stared down into the roots. There, underneath the thick cover of leaves and moss, was a person. He had been buried deep in the ground, although the shifting of time had brought his body up through the soft earth. His hair was stuck to the tree, growing into the moss as though he were part of it. Even some of his skin had attached itself to the bark, turning green and brown with age. But his eyes were still vivid blue, even though tiny sprouts of grass were growing where his eyelashes should be.

"Hello," she whispered. Freya hoped her horror didn't come through in her tones.

"You shouldn't be here," he said again, struggling for breath and heaving air back into his lungs.

She looked closer and realized there were twigs sticking through his torso. They created a mockery of a ribcage, and she imagined struggling to breathe was difficult. Hence the wheezing tones of his words. "I didn't have a choice," she belatedly replied.

"Ah." He forced more air through his throat. "The trees wanted you here, then."

The trees suddenly seemed far more ominous than before. She was afraid of them now, if this was what they wanted to do to visitors.

"Why are you here?" she asked. "It seems like a poor resting place for one such as you."

"Such as me?" the creature looked down at itself then back at her. "Oh, missing limbs and all. I suppose that does look a little... strange."

Strange wasn't even the word for it. She didn't know if she would even consider him to be alive. Magic was strange. A forest that moved on its own. That was strange. But a man stuck to a tree with moss growing all over his body, or at least what parts of his body that she could see?

That wasn't strange. That was a nightmare come to life as she talked with a corpse.

"Um." Freya glanced over her shoulder at her father, who was still pacing in his cage. When she made eye contact with him, he snapped his jaws. And he was entirely a wolf at this point. There was no cursed figure, which she thought was maybe a good thing.

Was she supposed to talk with this dead man about how to get her father out? Maybe that's what the forest wanted. She was supposed to ask her questions here and now, and that would get her pointed in the right direction.

Freya really didn't want to. The heaving sound of his breath terrified her, and she knew it would stick in her dreams for months to come.

Staring up at the sky, she watched the light filter through the branches over her head and chewed on her lips. She'd always said there was no time to waste when she had to get something done. After all, a hero didn't hesitate. A hero charged forward to help.

"Am I supposed to speak with you about getting my father back?" she asked.

"Maybe." The man shifted again. This time, she watched as he lifted an arm out of the moss. Giant mushroom caps grew from his bicep down to his elbow, though the appendage was very thin and almost mummified. "The trees talk through me, sometimes."

"Are there more like you?"

"Hundreds." He met her gaze with those horrible blue eyes. "You didn't notice all of us?"

All of them? She turned her gaze back to the forest and this time, yes, she saw all the bodies. One for each tree. People growing into the bark, into roots, tangled in moss. Some of them were so much a part of their tree that their skin had turned rough and ashen. A few of them lifted their arms when they saw her looking at them, beckoning for her to come forward and speak with them as well.

Magic pulsed in her heart and told her to stay right where

she was. Now was the moment where danger ran hot. She had to stay safe, and that meant speaking with the only tree who mattered.

She looked back to the giant she stood beside, the one who had nearly died to create a prison out of its own body. "You wanted to see me, didn't you?"

The tree shuddered. The body at the base of its roots suddenly quaked as though having a seizure. The man's eyes closed, and his mouth opened wide. His lips didn't move at all as another voice spoke through him. It was the ancient sound of a madman and a healer all wrapped in one. Deep and echoing through the throat of the dead man. "I did."

"Why?" She tried very hard not to shiver in disgust.

"Poison spreads through the Summer Court. A monstrous poison that cannot be contained by any root or poultice we make. You must help us." A small green beetle crawled out of the man's mouth, shook its body, and then flew off into the golden light of day.

Freya swallowed hard. "What can I do to help? I'm just a mortal."

"You're more than that. You're this changeling's child and he came to us seeking help. As the wolves did in the old days." Perhaps the tree sought her out because it didn't have leverage on anyone else. Freya was the only one it could speak with at this point in time. Whatever the reason, the trees knew they had her by the throat.

She would do anything to help her father. Even make a deal with a forest.

Sighing, Freya nodded. "If I find out what is harming the Summer Court, will you let my father go?"

"I'll do better than that." The forest sighed with her, every tree shifting with a breeze that tangled in Freya's hair. "I will heal your father of his curse, but you must save the Summer Court from itself."

"Are you going to tell me what needs saving? Or why it's

poisoned?" Freya lifted her hands, knowing that she'd get no answers. "Perhaps who is poisoned or where that came from?"

The tree laughed, and the sound was horribly eerie coming out of a mouth that didn't move. "No, Freya. You've been in the faerie realms long enough to know that I will give you no help at all. Save us and I'll give your father back as he once was all those years ago."

Of course it couldn't be that easy. Freya turned to give her father one last look, but the forest warped and stretched again. The ground shifted underneath her feet and she had the awful sensation of something picking her up and throwing her through the air. Her stomach leapt into her throat and then she slammed down onto a cold seashell floor with balcony doors just behind her.

Birds chirped in her ears. The sun warmed her back. And the forest disappeared with the faint sound of laughter dancing in her ears.

She stood up carefully, wincing at the aching bruises on her knees from where she'd hit the balcony too hard. She dusted off her skirts and planted her hands on her hips. "That wasn't very friendly, you know!"

The doors behind her slammed open so hard the glass shattered. Freya whirled around to see a furious Goblin King standing in their bedroom.

"How dare you put yourself in danger like that?" he snarled. "Get in here."

CHAPTER 6

CHAPTER 6

O h, she was in so much trouble. The angry glower on his face didn't budge, even when she skirted past him into the room beyond.

Freya walked into their bedroom like a child who was about to get scolded by her parent. And she knew he had every right to do so. He didn't know where the portal had taken her, only that it didn't want her with him. No way to know if she was even alive. If that had happened in reverse, then Freya would have been an absolute mess.

He could yell at her all he wanted, she supposed. That was fair.

Freya sat down on the bed, tucked her hands underneath her bottom, and squeezed her shoulders up to her ears. She was ready to be shouted at, and he could take his time. However long it took for him to feel better, that was how long she would sit here and listen.

She heard the pounding of his footsteps as he started pacing across the room. Each thud mirrored her heartbeat. Eldridge lifted a finger, opened his mouth, then closed it again. He continued pacing and trying to speak for long moments before he finally sighed.

His long legs ate up the distance between them and he sank onto his knees before her. Gently, ever so gently, he laid his head down in her lap and surrounded her hips with his arms. "I thought I had lost you," he muttered. "That magic was old and powerful. I fought against it for hours and it didn't budge. I could have done that for centuries and not known if I would ever get you back, or just your corpse."

She shouldn't tell him about the dead things in the forest. And some other voice whispered in her mind that she shouldn't mention her father, either. Eldridge would want to rush into the trees and free her father, tearing this court down around their ears in the process.

They couldn't. This game had to be played the way the forest wanted, or they would all end up tangled in the roots like those other elves.

Freya combed her fingers through his hair, scraping his scalp with her nails and easing her fingers down the back of his neck. "I didn't die, you know. I was fine."

"Yes, I see that. But I realized in the time that you were gone that the thought of losing you wrecks me. I couldn't use my magic in the right way. I couldn't even think about what would happen if you didn't return." He lifted his head, eyes more serious than she'd ever seen before. "You give me a reason to live, Freya. A reason to be a better version of myself."

"I'm sorry I made you so worried," she whispered. Freya traced his eyebrows with her fingers, following the strong, sharp lines to the edges of his eyes. "I wouldn't have taken the risk if there was any other way. I had to know what was happening."

"And what happened?"

"That place... Those trees." She swallowed hard. "They were the same trees that were behind our house, Eldridge. The same ones that were in the mortal realm."

His hands flexed on her hips and he lifted himself onto the

bed with her. Eldridge threaded his fingers together, pressed them to his lips, and frowned. "The same trees? My darling, that's not possible."

"Apparently it is. They even said they were. But they..." She paused, trying to figure out a lie that was not too far off from the truth. "They knew something about my father. Some detail that will solve all of this. They said they would tell us, but in return, we have to help the Summer Court."

Eldridge rolled his eyes in frustration. "Of course we do. It's never easy in the faerie realm, and apparently even the trees won't do anything for free. What do they want?"

"They said there's a poison spreading through the Summer Court. We have to find out what it is and how to stop it." She shook her head and frowned. "I'm not sure how clear that direction is, though. The Summer Court seems fine to me. It's exactly like it used to be."

It didn't seem that Eldridge felt the same way. His expression darkened, and he stood. He made his way to the balcony where he could stare out over the ocean beyond. "The Summer Court wasn't always like this. The elves weren't always faceless and searching for the next beautiful thing. The Lord was the one who helped people find themselves. They settled into what they should look like so they could understand themselves better. Finding a face was like finding your soul."

Perhaps that was why all those people who were stuck to the trees had faces, then. They were the older elves who had lived in a time that was gentler on their kind.

"Ah," she replied. "So maybe that's the poison?"

"It's too easy." He took a deep breath, shoulders moving with the slow movement. "There's only one person who would have felt a poison spreading through this land, and that would be the Lord himself. But he should have told me if there was something wrong here. No court leader is supposed to handle something like that on their own."

She stood up, followed him to the window. Freya put her

hand on his back and rubbed the tension there. "But you two have a strained relationship at best. Perhaps he didn't feel comfortable talking to you."

"Perhaps not." He reached an arm out for her, tucking Freya against his side and holding her close. Eldridge pressed a kiss to the top of her head. "Very few people actually liked me until you."

"Is that so?" She smiled against his side, listening to the beat of his heart against her ear. "I can't imagine why."

He snorted. "Right, I'm sure you can't. But we may as well take our chances while we can. Look." He pointed below them toward the sands that spread out toward the sea.

The Summer Lord strode across the white sand beach with three elves trailing along behind him. His bright white suit almost blended into the setting, but he was relatively alone and yes, this was a great opportunity for them to speak with him. No guards to stop them. Other than the one at their door, that was.

She looked up at Eldridge and lifted a brow. "The question is how we're going to get out there before he leaves. The guard was much larger than most elves. I know you're powerful, Eldridge, but he's pretty big."

"First of all, I don't appreciate the suggestion that I couldn't fight someone much larger than me." He scowled at her. "Second, what makes you think I planned on walking?"

"Well, most people do need to walk. It's not like we can float through the air." She regretted saying the words as soon as they came out of her mouth.

Eldridge tightened his grip on her and his face twisted with a mad smile. "Oh, my darling, I so enjoy proving you wrong."

His magic whipped around them, hugging her tightly and dragging her off the balcony. Eldridge walked through the air like it was solid. He strode without purpose or haste, just a few steps here and there while he watched her expression change from horror, to fear, and then laughter as Freya finally let go and realized they would not plummet to their death.

They strolled like a couple who had done this a thousand times before. Like they were walking beside a pretty river and he was pointing out a view for her to admire.

Eldridge nudged her to look to their left. "That's where Leo and I used to hide from his parents. Dreadful people. They were so stuffy and we always wanted to go on adventures. They wanted us to learn which fork to use."

The small building was likely used by the gardeners to store their tools. "A rather dangerous place for children to hide. How did you keep all your fingers and toes?"

He snorted. "The same way I do now. Practice and hoping no one notices if I lop one off and stick it back on with magic."

That fit her description of him quite nicely. Eldridge apparently had always been the kind of person to take the risk first and then wonder if it was the right decision later. She could imagine him as a little boy, running wild through the Summer Court with his dear friend at his side.

"I'm imagining you as a little terror," she said with a laugh. "How accurate is that?"

"People screamed when they heard my name." He smiled at her with a sharp-toothed grin. "They still do."

Yes, she was certain that was true as well. There were very few faeries who wanted to risk angering the Goblin King. The man was terrifying when he wanted to be.

They landed on the sand behind the group of elves and their Summer Lord. None of them appeared to notice the couple that had floated down from the sky, nor did they react when the two of them started walking nearer.

"Leo!" Eldridge called out.

The Summer Lord flinched so hard that he almost fell onto the sands. He righted himself and spun around with an angry glare. "You're supposed to be in your room!"

The thunderous sound of his voice was impressive. Even the sea seemed terrified of the Summer Lord, because the waves froze for a moment before they kissed the shore once again.

Each elf retreated to a safe distance away from their Lord. Freya wondered if that was a warning. Was this court leader known for exploding? Considering how much she'd seen him drinking when she was here, she wouldn't be surprised if he did.

His anger ruled his actions rather than logic. And it was such a shame, because he really was handsome. Someone had braided his hair tight to his head, and the long tails looked like that of a squid that flung around him as he moved. The sheer amount of time it would have taken to make him look like that made her think him even more attractive. The golden buttons on his suit gleamed in the sun. Tiny aquamarine gemstones were inlaid in each button.

"Yes," Eldridge replied, looking at his fingers as though he were already bored with the conversation. "You know I don't like being locked up. I get too bored."

"I don't care if you're bored," the Summer Lord snarled. "I care that you stay where I put you. You're not allowed to wander through my court without an escort, Eldridge."

"Not allowed?" Eldridge lifted his brows in fake surprise. "I'm the Goblin King. There is no part of this court or any other that is off limits for me to visit. Or have you forgotten that?"

The Summer Lord's expression darkened. Clouds appeared over their head and Freya heard thunder in the distance. This faerie lord was extremely powerful. She wondered how close he had been to getting the Goblin throne himself.

And they didn't have time for the two of these men to butt heads yet again. She wanted to confront the Lord and get this over with.

Stepping in between them, she forced the Lord's attention onto her. "I met with the trees," she said.

Her voice rang through the air and suddenly the skies were bright blue again. The Lord stared at her with a shocked expression, mouth open and brows furrowed. "You what?" he asked in hushed tones.

"I met with the trees," she repeated. "They said I needed to help rid this land of a poison. And I think you know what that poison is. Let us help you, Leo. Take a step back from being the Summer Lord or having old prejudices. This isn't about us, anymore. This is about your court and the safety of your people."

He took a step away from her, shaking his head. "It's not possible." The horror in his expression told her everything she needed to know.

"The poison has affected you too, hasn't it?" She trailed him through the sands, matching his every step. "You know exactly what I'm talking about, and you haven't tried to stop it at all. Do you even want to stop it?"

"Eldridge," Leo growled. "Get your woman and make sure she stays away from me."

Freya felt the grip of the Goblin King on her arm, but she wasn't pausing now. She couldn't. Not when they were so close. "Tell us what it is and we might be able to help. Why wouldn't you want someone to help you?"

The Summer Lord lifted his hands, the rings on his fingers glowing with power. "Get her away from me before I do something I regret."

Without question, Eldridge scooped her up by the waist and dragged her away. "Freya, we'll talk to him another time."

She struggled, although she knew it was a waste of energy. "But he knows! Eldridge, he knows what I'm talking about. Let me go!"

The Summer Lord turned away from them and walked back down the sands. The elves looked between the three of them and then continued to follow their master. Though, this time they stayed a lot farther back.

When Eldridge finally released her, she whipped around with an angry snarl. "How dare you? I was so close!"

"To getting killed." He ran his fingers through his hair with a frustrated sound. "Listen to me. Leo has never been good at controlling his emotions. It's the main reason he didn't get the goblin throne when we were all competing for it. There's something missing from him. Compassion has never been his strong suit and if you had pushed him any farther, he would have killed you."

"With you standing right here?" She pursed her lips. "I doubt that."

"You shouldn't." The haze of a haunted memory ghosted over his features. "I've seen him do it before, Freya. Just because I'm standing here wouldn't stop him. And I don't know if I'm quick enough to prevent that gesture of anger from hitting you."

Well, that would make this all much more difficult if the Summer Lord refused to help them.

Tossing up her hands, she gave in. "Fine, then. If we can't talk with him about it, then what do we do next?"

He shrugged as if he didn't know the answer to that either. "I suppose we try to talk to the elves."

She stomped through the sand back toward the castle, muttering the entire time. "Talk to the elves. Like that will be so easy. None of the elves like to talk, and if they do, they only want to talk about dresses and parties. Talk to the elves. Sure. Let's see how far that gets us."

CHAPTER 7

Freya pinched the bridge of her nose and stared down at the small journal in her hand. She'd taken notes every time she talked with each elf, but that wasn't helpful at all.

This one had talked about the various plants that were in the Summer Kingdom for about an hour. And while these details would be interesting any other time of the year, she didn't really want to hear about this right now.

"Right," she repeated. "So I just want to clarify, please. We're asking about any poison you might feel in the area. A sickness, perhaps? Or maybe some of the plants you've taken care of happened to have died recently?"

The elf tapped a finger to its butterfly mask, then shook its head. "No. I don't think I've seen any of that."

"Really?" Freya pushed a little with this one because she couldn't believe that no one had seen any sign of poison. "Not a single note of concern in any area of the entire court?"

The elf shook its head and shrugged. "We're quite happy here. It's the best court to live in, you see. Summer is the most comfortable season, and the Summer Lord is a wonderful ruler. I'm happier than a clam."

Freya just didn't believe it. She couldn't imagine any of these people were happy when there was something insidious growing within their court. There had to be something someone wasn't telling her.

But that person wouldn't be the elf standing before her. She snapped the journal shut and gave the creature a sharp nod. "Thank you for talking with me. It's been a pleasure."

The elf waved and walked away, back into the lush greenery that it had been grooming. A few leaves stuck out of the elf's hair, and Freya had the distinct impression that they were actually growing out of the elf's head.

That one would end up in the forest before long, a voice whispered in her head. Soon it would be absorbed, just like the others.

Shivering, she stood up and walked back toward the castle where the others should be waiting for her. They had all split up to talk with as many elves as they could. All she could hope was that one of them had found out more information than she had.

Both Arrow and Eldridge stood to the side of the castle, nearer to an area that was currently undergoing construction. The gardens had all been ripped up, and none of the elves would go near it until someone had finally planted something there. Freya just wasn't sure who was supposed to do the planting.

She tromped up to them and waved the journal in her hand. "I've got absolutely nothing. It's like all the elves in this place lost their brains out their ears. Not a single one is aware of any poison, anything spreading, and all of them say they're perfectly happy. Why in the world would I want to meddle?"

Eldridge held up his own pale white leather notebook and grimaced. "I'm afraid my experience has been much the same. The elves aren't interested in talking to us, if they have any idea what's going on at all."

She turned toward their only hope, the little goblin dog who always wiggled underneath people's skin. "Please, Arrow, tell me you found out something about the curse affecting this court?"

His ears went straight up and he took a deep breath as though he were about to tell them the greatest information of the century. But then his ears flattened to his skull again, and he tucked his tail between his legs. "I'm afraid not, Miss Freya. The elves wouldn't even talk to me. It's like they live in a different version of this court than we see."

Freya puffed a breath at the hair in front of her face and wished there was something stiff to drink. "Of course they wouldn't," she grumbled.

The elves were loyal to their Summer Lord. Freya and her companions were utter strangers, and they stood out among the crowd. If they wanted to get information out of these people, then they needed to seem like they were one of them.

Or find out information from the Summer Lord himself. But that seemed even less likely.

She tucked her journal into her pocket and crossed her arms firmly over her chest. "Well, do either of you have any ideas?"

Both Eldridge and Arrow shared a look, then turned back to her with blank expressions. Freya was so tired of doing everything, especially when she had no idea where to go with this one. Staring out into the pavilion and the beautiful gardens beyond, she finally just shrugged.

That was it, then.

She'd failed her mother. Her father would remain trapped in those trees, and she would be stuck here. Trying to mend the bond between a family that had lost a very dear member.

Her father used to swing her up over his head until she screamed in the sunlight. Freya remembered him as an overly large man with a laugh that boomed like thunder. He was too loud. Too opinionated. Everyone had thought him to be a bear of a person, but they'd still liked him.

It was hard not to like her father. He had a pure heart and that shone through everything he did.

Arrow stepped forward and tucked his nose underneath her

hand. "There's one more person who might help us. I don't know if she'll answer, but…"

Eldridge snapped his fingers forcefully. "Arrow, you genius! Why didn't I think of that?"

"Of what?" Freya looked between the two of them, trying to guess who they might be talking about. "We already know the Summer Lord won't give us a hint at all."

"But there was another person who stayed with us every summer I visited here." Eldridge's eyes glowed with excitement. "I need a pool of water. Come on, you two."

He raced away before Freya could get anything else out of him. Arrow was quick to follow, and if she didn't hurry, then they would both leave her in the dust. She tilted her head back to stare up at the clouds above them. "I don't understand a thing about these two," she muttered. "Why can't they just tell me what's going on before they race off into the distance?"

Shaking her head, she ran after them through the lush forest beyond. Freya slapped large monstera leaves out of her way and tried her best not to step on the flower gardens that the other two were so carelessly trudging through. The elves were still dangerous and territorial about their land. The last thing she wanted was to make these masked creatures angry enough to hunt her and her companions down.

She burst through the undergrowth out into a small glenn in the middle of this terrifying garden. A vernal pool waited in the center, tiny clusters of algae and lily pads making the edges difficult to tell what ground was solid. Some of the earth disappeared into the aquamarine waters.

Eldridge stood at the edge, holding out his hand above the water. He squeezed his eyes shut and muttered words she couldn't quite hear.

A furry paw stopped her from stepping any closer. "Don't interrupt him when he's casting spells," Arrow said. "We wouldn't want the whole thing to go awry and then end up with our feet as hands."

Freya didn't want to know if that was actually a concern. She didn't plan to risk it.

They both waited and watched the Goblin King as he worked. He moved his hands in strange patterns over the waters, muttering those words in a certain cadence that started to sound like a song. The more she listened, the more Freya wanted to walk closer to him. To step into the pool of bubbling pond water...

"Freya," Arrow hissed. "He's almost done. Just stop moving, would you?"

She snapped out of it and suddenly, Eldridge stopped speaking. He spread his fingers wide and dark magic sank into the water from his fingers. It spread through the very air like drops of ink, and the pool stopped bubbling. All sound in the glen silenced as the water turned into a solid mirror.

Freya gulped. What had the Goblin King done with his magic?

Eldridge held out his hand, gesturing for her to step up to his side. "Come here, Freya. I want you to look at this."

Had he created some way in the water to see the future? Freya wasn't sure she'd ever want to see that. The future was meant to be unknown and if she knew it, then would it ever come to pass?

Yet her feet brought her to his side without argument. Eldridge slid his arm around her waist and tugged her to the mossy edge of the pool. Their reflections were perfect on the glassy surface. And then he lifted a hand and pointed. "Look."

Just behind their image, another appeared. Horns silhouetted against the sky, and a bell skirt swaying around her hips, the Autumn Thief was lovely as ever. She wore bright red lip paint today, and her eyes were dramatically ringed with kohl.

Freya looked behind them. But the Thief wasn't in the glen. She was only in the water. "How is that possible?" she asked.

"Magic," the Thief replied with a laugh. "You've forgotten how much is possible, my dear. And how little you know."

A knot of tension eased in her stomach at the sound of the Autumn Thief's voice. Somehow, this woman always made Freya feel safe. No matter what circumstance they were in.

Freya glanced over at Arrow. "This was your plan? Ask for help from the Thief?"

"She knows more than most." He trotted to their side and stood up on his back legs. With a sheepish smile, he waved into the pool. "Hello, darling."

"Arrow. I see you've at least been able to dress to your standard on this adventure." The Thief crossed her arms over her chest and glared at them severely. "I was busy, Eldridge. You know I cannot be summoned without warning. There's too much to do here."

"Yes, yes." He dismissed her words with a wave of his hand. "Whatever you need to do can wait. We've something a little more important to deal with here."

Freya rolled her eyes at the same time as the Thief. "Eldridge," she scolded. "Just because we have issues here doesn't mean the Thief's are any less important. We thank you for your time, Thief. Really. We didn't know who else to turn to."

A breeze kicked up and swirled the skirts around the Thief's legs. She nodded, and a small green snake curved around one of her horns. "Then how can I help?"

Eldridge was quick to answer this time, and Freya supposed he was the one who knew best how to ask questions. "Do you remember when we were young and used to spend our summer here?"

"Of course I do." The Thief shrugged. "I was a very different person then, but that doesn't mean I have banished the memories from my mind."

"Good. Because apparently there's a poison spreading through these lands, and I have a gut feeling it has to do with something we saw when we were here. In the isles after all that time." He shook his head. "There's something warning me to look further, deeper into our history, but I cannot put my finger on why. Or how."

"Might I suggest that's because you and the Summer Lord were always running around seeking out new adventures? You wouldn't remember something important if it bit you in the ass, because you would find the next thing to bite in the same spot." The Thief heaved a sigh and then pointedly stared at Freya. "You're the one who took this on, you know. You must have the patience of a saint to deal with this one."

"To be fair, I don't really know what I'm getting into," Freya replied with a laugh.

"Hm." The Thief turned her attention back to the Goblin King with pursed lips. "I don't know everything you're looking for, but I remember that we found a book that warned the Summer Lord could grow ill. And it wasn't something he could catch, but was entirely related to the forest. Remember?"

"Not really." Eldridge's hand flexed on Freya's hip and he stepped away from her. Closer to the pool so he could see the Thief easier. "Was it a book that you and I found?"

"A scroll. Some story on it had said the Summer Lord wasn't the true ruler of this court. That he never would be, because the forest and the plants make the decisions for the Summer Court. I remember Leo was horribly upset about it." She turned her face from them, clearly listening to someone they couldn't see. "I don't have a lot more time, my dear. All I can say is that I know the forest can take back the right to rule its court if it's disappointed in the Lord. That's as good a place to start as I can think of."

The pool shuddered with a wind that brushed over the surface, and then the Autumn Thief was gone. All three of them stared into the shimmering, algae tinted water as if she might return.

Freya was the first to speak. "Well, that settles it."

Her two companions looked at her as if she'd grown a second head. Eldridge cleared his throat and asked, "Settles what?"

"I have to go back to the forest, clearly. It didn't give me all the answers I need to figure this all out. And if the forest is disappointed in the Summer Lord, then I need to figure out why." She shrugged. "Disappointment is one thing, but poisoning the entire court because it's upset with a single person? That's just immature."

Eldridge lunged toward her and slapped his hand over her mouth. Frantically, he stared up at the trees, eyes wide and flicking through the canopy. "She didn't mean it. She's just a mortal and has no idea what you listen to. Please don't punish her for ignorance."

What was he talking about? Freya glared at him, wiggling to get out of his grip.

Finally, she pulled herself away from him and took a deep breath of anger. "Excuse you! Eldridge."

"I'm not saying you shouldn't," he rushed to say, holding his hands up for peace. "Just... Be a little more careful about the words you choose. Would you?"

She supposed he might be right. After all, if she was going to converse with those trees again, she needed to have her wits about her.

CHAPTER 8

Their bedroom filled with dread as Freya readied herself to return to the forest. Even she was starting to get a little nervous.

Eldridge held her face in his hands and squeezed a little too tight. "Be careful."

"I plan on it," she replied with a soft laugh. "You don't have to worry so much, you know. I made it there and back the last time without a scratch."

He pressed his lips to her forehead, drawing her in for another long hug. "Yes, I know you did. I hope that the forest doesn't want to hurt you, and that it won't think this second visit, uninvited might I add, is the opportunity to amend its previous mistake."

Freya didn't think the forest would mind at all. After all, it was keeping her father locked away from her and her family. And it wanted to heal her father. It had made that very clear.

But Eldridge didn't know that her father was in that magical forest, locked away in a prison made of roots. She should have told him by now. The same voice kept whispering in her ear that now wasn't the time to tell Eldridge. He was rushing too much through this quest, as he usually did. His attention to detail just wasn't there yet. Soon, she could admit that she already knew where her father was. Not yet, though.

She pulled away from his grip and nodded. "I'm going to be fine, you know. Nothing bad is going to happen. I'm going to get more information out of the trees, then I'll be right back here and ready to take on more questions with you. All right?"

He stepped away from her, but the expression of worry never left his face. He didn't think this trip would be as easy as the first. That much was clear in his expression. "All right. Just..."

She smiled. "Be careful. I know, my Goblin King will be worrying on the other side of this door."

"And if you think for even an instant that the forest wants to hurt you, call to me."

If it wanted to hurt her, then no one was getting through that portal until it was finished with her. Freya didn't have to understand magic better to know that without question.

Still, she nodded to make him feel better about the whole situation. If she could ease his worry with her false bravado, then so be it.

Freya turned toward the balcony doors and put her hands on the bronze knobs. She did exactly as Eldridge had told her to do. Envision the doors opening into the forest where she wanted to go. She'd already been there, so this kind of portal should be very easy. All she had to do was let the magic do what it wanted to do.

And he'd insisted her magic wanted to help her. That was the function of having magic, or at least that's what he claimed. It would bring her from the Summer Court and into that secret place, if only she would let it.

The magic uncoiled deep in her belly. She'd finally given it a personality or a visage inside herself. Freya imagined her magic like a snake that twisted through her veins. Sometimes it was nice and only wanted to be held high in the sun. Other times, the magic wanted nothing more than to bite down hard on someone else.

She exhaled and opened the doors. Freya didn't open her eyes until she felt the soft breeze on her face and smelled the dark, earthy scent of moss and wood.

Blinking, she stared up into the golden sun and smiled. It had worked. If only she could turn around and tell Eldridge that he'd been right. She would have enjoyed sharing this moment with her Goblin King, who so loved teaching her how to use her magic.

Instead, she was alone with the trees.

Or rather, not so alone. This time, the bodies were far more evident, each of them reaching out for her with their mossy hands and bony fingers. She strode by them very carefully, making sure none of them caught hold of her pale yellow skirts. They would drag her into their prison with them. She was certain of it.

Even the trees seemed more sinister this time. They loomed over her head and their branches were too heavy with moss. Dripping wet plops of green down on her shoulders and head.

"I'm here to ask questions," she said firmly. "You will not frighten me away."

The forest shook with a sound that was almost laughter. Like the trees thought her bravery was adorable, but that she would not get far with that kind of ridiculous thought. She was just a mortal in a forest of ancient trees who could tear her limb from limb if they wanted to. Even the roots were rolling in the ground. They were ready to pull her into the moss where she would stay forever.

Freya carefully picked her way over the wet ground and headed to the same tree where she knew her father was. The giant tree that was hidden behind gates because apparently someone had thought the beast was dangerous enough to keep under lock and key.

Although, she didn't know where that key was.

Dust motes swirled in the air like tiny glowing faeries lighting her way. It was almost beautiful enough to make her forget the bodies that were still dragging themselves closer to her. They reached with skeletal fingers, trying to touch the trailing edge of her skirt.

No, she wouldn't focus on the dead things. The forest was trying to scare her away, and though it could do its best to try, she would not allow it to have space in her mind. Fear had no place here.

She walked through the iron gates and into the glen where the tree grew. It was larger than she remembered, or perhaps she was looking at it through a healthy amount of fear. Either way, she knew to tread more carefully now.

"I have questions," she called out again. "And I would like to see my father. Please."

Freya threw the last word into the air, hoping the tree would see she didn't mean any harm. She wasn't demanding for its attention. She was a girl looking to see her father one more time.

The tree heaved another sigh, and suddenly, the dead man in the roots came to life again. He opened his eyes and yawned, then met her gaze with one as green as the leaves above them. "You shouldn't have come back here without an invitation, girl."

"I know that." She stepped closer, holding up her hands. "But I had to know you were making good on your own bargain. I had to know he was doing better, or at least that my father was still alive."

"You don't trust us?"

No. Of course she didn't trust the trees. Freya frowned at the question and tried very hard to find words that weren't insulting. But her answer couldn't be dulled when she only had sharp anger in her chest.

"No," she replied. "I don't trust you at all. I think you have your own reasons for calling me here, and that I would be a fool to ignore that truth."

The man's face twisted with mirth. He opened that cavernous mouth and laughed. A tooth fell from his skull into the moss that covered the remains of his legs. "I had forgotten how lovely it was to see a mortal brimming with honesty. You're smart to not trust us, but you are also a fool for coming here. What a strange mixture brews inside that head of yours."

Freya didn't think she was all that strange. Most people were intelligent, but they made foolish decisions all the time. Usually in the name of love. As she was doing now.

She took a step toward the prison of roots. "May I see my father, please?"

"Do you think he'll be so changed? He was nothing more than a wolf when you saw him last, child." The man in the moss grinned, his eyes still wild and teeth glowing bone white in the moss of his skull.

Freya thought about how to answer that one. She could lie and question the tree's integrity. Perhaps making it angry would get her what she wanted faster. But Eldridge's words still rung in her head. Sometimes she didn't have to fight with another to get what she wanted. Maybe she could ask for it.

"I do think you'll have changed him. You love him as much as I do, although I don't understand why. Was he a child in these forests? Was that when you first met him?" She took another step toward the prison where the tree was keeping her father. "He's a very good man, I know that. And I can only imagine you had some part in ensuring he grew up like that."

The dead man sighed. He closed his eyes, and she thought for a moment that the tree would let her go to her father. Instead, he talked with his eyes closed. Like he was remembering the past. "He was a good little boy. Where the other faerie children ran through the forest without care, he picked up sticks in their wake and lay them back in our roots. He used to think if things broke off of our branches, that we would miss them until they came back to us. A kind heart in that one."

Freya smiled. That was exactly how she remembered her father. He took the time to notice the little things that made other people's lives easier.

She inched to the side until she was right in front of the cage. Peering into the shadows beyond, she could see him standing. Though this time he was in that strange form, mixed man and beast, she knew that meant he was a little more like himself.

"Look at that," she whispered. "You were healing him the whole time."

"I wasn't going to let him rot in there. He never liked being a wolf." The tree shook its branches over her head and a rainfall of leaves dusted the prison. The thick layer hid her father from her gaze. "Now you are going to ask me your question and leave. Too much stimulation would only make him turn back into the wolf and then all our work will be for nothing."

She wanted to see more of her father. Just a little. Every glimpse healed a painful ache in her chest that wouldn't go away, no matter how hard she tried to ignore it.

But she wasn't here to see her father.

Not yet, at least.

"I spoke with a friend to figure out what the poison in this land might be. You've been going to great lengths to hide that information from me." She turned back to the man tangled in roots, planting her hands on her hips and hoping she looked like her mother when it was time to scold the children. "If you want my help, why are you doing everything in your power to hide the truth?"

"A quest, once given, cannot be made easy." The tree said the words like they were something she should have known. As if everyone in the faerie realms knew that this was the truth. Plain and simple.

Freya furrowed her brows. "That's not the way of it, though. If you want to change things, then why wouldn't you help?"

"The rules of the game have always been clear, Freya."

Clear as mud, as they were.

"Fine," she grumbled. "I want to at least be clear. I know you're the one who caused all this pain and suffering. The poison you spoke about is erupting from the very trees, and that I don't appreciate not knowing this from the start."

The man shifted, lifting an arm and pointing at her. "You're smarter than you look, Miss Freya."

She hummed low and under her breath, but nodded her thanks. "You're unhappy with the way the Summer Lord is ruling this court. That much is very obvious. But I want to know why."

This perked up the man in the tree. He moved his bony arms, his whole body shifting and rolling with moss that grew and died within blinks. He rose to the trunk of the tree, still stuck to the bark and hanging limp. Somehow, he was ominous to look at. "The Summer Lord mocks this court with his parties and his drink and his foolish nature. He knows what we've asked of him. He knows exactly what he has to do to make this throne his. And until then, I will continue to eat away at his court until it is buried beneath my roots. The age of the elf is coming to an end, and he knows how to stop my reckoning."

A chill swept down Freya's spine as he finished the speech. If this tree wanted to murder everyone in this court, she didn't question that it could. This wasn't just a forest, this was a creature who was living and breathing. Through dead things, sure, but still alive in some way.

"I understand," she said, ducking her head low. "My only challenge to you is to understand that no one can fix something they don't know is broken."

"Oh, he knows," the tree snarled. "He is aware of what he has done. The Summer Lord continues to refuse our requests. If you want to know as well, then I will tell you this. Go to the isles off the coast. The ones he told your Goblin King that no one travels to any longer. See the truth for yourself."

Freya shivered, fearing for her life and that of her father's as well. "Thank you," she whispered. "I am very grateful for your assistance in this quest you've sent me on."

"Please." The man drifted down the trunk and landed back in the mossy roots. "You are not a meek creature, and it doesn't look good on your frame. Pick your chin up and be the terrifying woman I first met. The one who I knew could turn this court around if she wished to."

At least the compliment boded well for later on. Freya nodded firmly and turned to leave. She squared her shoulders and forced herself to look brave as she wandered past those dead things that wanted to clutch onto her. She kept her chin up even as she reached the doors that would lead her back to her private rooms in the Summer Court.

But inside, she was so frightened that all she could hear was her own screams.

CHAPTER 9

"You think the trees want to help us?" Eldridge shook his head while he flipped the covers back on their bed. "I really don't think they want to do anything like that, Freya. They aren't giving beings, if you hadn't noticed."

"Oh, I noticed." She pulled her hair from its braid and let it fall loose down her back.

Now that they were sleeping in the same bed consistently, she'd taken to letting her hair get wild. As much as she hated the long length of it getting tangled, she very much enjoyed waking up every morning and having Eldridge there to brush it for her. And he liked brushing it. Every morning they got up and had their own little routine to start the day.

He frowned and punched his pillow, fluffing it for the night. "Why do you think they want us to go to the islands?"

"We've already been over this multiple times. I don't know why." She crawled onto her side of the bed and motioned for him to get in with her. "But arguing about it repeatedly will not get any more information into our heads."

"I think if we talk through it, we might at least be able to understand why the trees are so frustrated." He glared at her.

Oh, he was so handsome. Freya loved it when he glared at her like that. His brows furrowed in the same way they did when he was in the throes of passion. Not that she'd ever tell him that. His ego was already too big.

One last time, she waggled her fingers for him to get into bed. "We can't do much more until the morning, Eldridge. Even if we both bang our heads against the walls. I don't think we're going to figure this one out. The trees said go to the isles. I don't see another choice. Do you?"

He grumbled but crawled into bed with her. Hand over hand, he dragged himself closer and dramatically fell on top of her.

All the breath whooshed from her lungs. She curled her arms around him, holding his head close to her heart, but she still wheezed, "Was that necessary?"

"Yes. You disagreed with me and I don't like it," he muttered, his mouth mashed against her neck. "You don't have to be right all the time, you know."

"Yes, I do," she replied with a laugh. "Otherwise no one would ever be right, and then where would we be?"

Eldridge curved his arms around her, holding her as tightly as she was holding him. "I suppose we'd be in the same place as we currently are, my love. Fumbling around in the dark because damn trees won't tell us where to go next."

She laughed, bouncing his head on her chest with the sound of her mirth. "Eldridge! We know where we have to go next. We have to go to the isles, because that's where the trees told us to go."

"And we can't go there without the Summer Lord's permission." He pressed a kiss to her throat. "Which means tomorrow we have to beg him to give us that permission."

"Ah." And she assumed that wouldn't be all that easy. "What are the chances of him saying yes without asking questions?"

"Zero to none." He pressed another kiss to her skin, this time lingering on her jaw. "But I don't want to talk about him right now."

A blush spread across her body and suddenly she didn't want to talk about the Summer Lord either. She wanted to focus on the Goblin King in her bed, who commanded every ounce of her attention. "Oh," she whispered, cupping the back of his head and drawing him up her body. "What do you want to talk about then?"

"Nothing," he growled against her lips. "Nothing at all."

It took them a very long time to fall asleep.

The next morning, Freya felt like she was walking on clouds. She'd spent the night in his arms, in the most warm and wonderful place they'd traveled to so far, and the sun was shining. She stretched her arms over her head, reveling in the sunlight on her body. Finally, this was a place in the faerie realm where she would stay for a while.

"Up!" Eldridge's voice sliced through the air. "We don't have time for you to be lazy this morning."

Well, that would ruin the mood in a heartbeat. Why wouldn't they have time? They knew what they had to do today. She'd spoken with the trees and they were healing her father step by step. Why couldn't she enjoy herself for a morning?

Grumbling, she sat up in bed with her hair wild around her face. Blowing at one of the frizzy strands, she watched as he paced from one end of the room to the other. Eldridge lifted his hands up and down, summoning things as he went.

A vanity appeared directly across from her with a sparkling cushion that was clearly from his own court. Then dresses popped into view to her right. Too many of them to count, but they were all hung rather daintily on their hangers. Another crackle of magic revealed a stand that was where she should get her makeup done, considering the many pots of paint and rouge.

"What is all this?" she asked, stunned that he could bring so many things into their room with so little thought.

His magic was impressive. And she wondered if there was a limit to his abilities.

"This is everything we will need to get you ready to talk with the Summer Lord." He paused and stared at her with a critical eye. "Leo only likes pretty things, and if you aren't up to his standards, then you won't get the permission we need out of him."

"Excuse me." She stood and stretched her arms up over her head with another yawn. "Why am I the one who's convincing him to help us? Shouldn't that be your job?"

"Absolutely not." He snapped his fingers and the remnants of her nightgown disappeared from her body. "I cannot lie, but you can. Thus, the only logical conclusion is that you will lie to him and say we want to go to the island to spend a little time with each other. Alone. Far away from the prying eyes of the elves. He will give us permission, and then we'll be on our merry way without him being any the wiser."

Right, because that was so much easier than telling the truth.

Freya lifted a brow. "Then why aren't you magicking me pretty like you've done so many times before?"

"Because the Summer Lord will notice that I've done that, and then he will get suspicious. We can't do anything that would make him question our intentions. He must believe that we want to get away for a while because we are desperately and wonderfully in love." He gestured with a hand and a sheer robe floated over to her. "Now, put this on."

She took the robe and stepped into it while still rolling her eyes. "That shouldn't be too hard to pretend that we're in love."

"Shouldn't it?" He paused in his spell casting to stare at her with eyes that saw right through her. "I would have thought it would be a little difficult for you. Considering you haven't said the words yet."

That stung. She knew she should have said them. Freya also was certain that she loved him with every fiber of her being. But that didn't make saying the words easier.

Freya tightened the ties around her waist and blew out a long breath. "I don't want to say it too early."

"We basically live together and sleep in the same bed every

night. How much more serious do you want it to be?" Eldridge pinched the bridge of his nose, then shook his hand in the air. "No, wait, don't answer that. I'm not pressuring you to say the words before you're ready. That is not who I am."

Freya wanted to reassure him. She wanted to say that she intended to say them when the time was right, but...

Well. She didn't know what was holding her back.

But she knew that she shouldn't take this long. That their relationship was as important, if not more important, than finding her father. She had to take the time to tell the Goblin King how she felt.

Freya opened her mouth and resolved to let the words pour out, even if she wasn't quite ready to say them. "Eldridge—"

He lunged forward and put his hand over her lips. "I'm not rushing you. I don't want to remember this moment for the rest of our days as the time when I pulled those words from your lips. Listen to me, Freya. I will wait a century if I must to hear you say the words that I so desperately want to hear. A thousand days, a thousand lifetimes, the wait would be worth it." He let his hand drop from her lips and gave her a wry smile. "But not a moment longer than that, my love. A man has his limits, after all."

She smiled and tried to remind herself that this was all right. She shouldn't feel rushed to tell him how she felt, even though she knew the feelings were mutual.

Freya sat down at the vanity table he'd set up, ready to prepare her makeup, and placed her hands on the wooden top so she wouldn't meddle with his design. "I do feel that way, you know. I don't know what's holding me back from saying it."

Eldridge approached her from behind, his expression calm in the mirror. He put his hands on her shoulders and squeezed. "I know you do, Freya. Otherwise, I wouldn't be waiting around for so long. I know when I'm not wanted, and you? You want me more than breath."

"Well, that's a little arrogant."

"We share the same vice." He leaned down to peck a kiss to her cheek, then grabbed his weapons of choice. Brandishing a brush at her, he started in on creating a perfect woman who would tempt the Summer Lord, and yet still be strong enough for the other elves to not mess with her.

Maybe it would take a lot of work, Freya didn't know. The last time she'd been here, all she had done was put on a fluffy dress and run out with the other elves.

But then again, last time the Summer Lord had known the elves he summoned to his dance were going to tempt the Goblin King. Perhaps this Lord had different tastes. And the longer Eldridge worked on setting her figure and features to right, the more she realized just how difficult it would be to please this Summer Lord.

The makeup changed the very shape of her features. He made her nose thinner, her cheekbones higher, and the hollows a little deeper. Her jaw suddenly appeared sharp enough to cut, and the wings he put on her eyes in dark kohl made her eyelashes look much longer. Eldridge even spent a ridiculous amount of time carving out the shape of her brows until they were so pointed, they almost touched her temples.

Then he set about on her hair, smoothing it down with a warmed pole that he'd set in the fire. The metal shape allowed him to create perfect, soft curls that she'd never be able to create on her own.

How in the world had he made her look like another person? She turned this way and that in the mirror, then made a tsking sound. "I don't even look like myself."

"No, you don't. But that's the point." He pointed to the rack of dresses. "Pick one."

"Oh, I get to choose what dress I wear? What if I wanted to show up like this?" She lifted her arms in the sheer fabric robe. "If we're selling my looks to the Summer Lord, wouldn't this intrigue him?"

"You aren't seducing him," Eldridge snarled. "I know you're trying to get a rise out of me, and it's working. Pick a dress."

Freya was goading him, but he was really enjoying this process a little too much. Knowing that this was what the fae thought of as pretty stung. Freya wasn't going to waste time every morning doing this to make herself presentable for him. She couldn't.

She walked over to the dress rack and picked the first one her eyes landed on. It was the color of seafoam and summer. A pale green with blue edges that fluffed like the tide kissing the land. The deep neckline pointed to her navel, but the rest of the dress was very modest. It clung to her form, certainly. But the sleeves were long, and the skirt touched the ground. Yet again, this was something Freya would never wear on her own. She wasn't this woman. At least, she wasn't sure that she was.

But she'd admit it felt amazing when Eldridge stared. His eyes heated with passion and his jaw dropped a bit before he shook himself.

"Wow," Eldridge whispered. "You look amazing."

"Thank you." She lifted her arms and did a tiny spin for him to get a good look. "Do you think I can convince the Summer Lord to let us go to the isles while I'm dressed like this?"

"I think you could convince him to kneel at your feet and worship the ground you walk on." Eldridge closed the distance between them and tugged her against him.

One arm banded around her waist like a bar of steel. The other he lifted to scoop his hand into her hair and hold her firmly in place for a kiss that stole her breath away. He branded her with his lips, teeth, and tongue. Like he was trying to remind her that no other faerie would ever satisfy her as he did.

Freya wouldn't deny that. The Goblin King was the only man she wanted and the only one who haunted every waking moment of her dreams.

She was breathless when they parted. Her words shook

slightly even as she resolved herself to focusing on the task. "Well, then."

He grinned, lips bright red. "Is that all you have to say?"

"I'll find my words by the time I speak with the Summer Lord." Freya stepped away and hoped she wasn't lying.

The longer she was around the Goblin King, the harder it was to focus on anything other than him.

CHAPTER 10

"Freya," Eldridge grabbed her arm just as they were leaving the castle. "Wait a moment, please. There's something I want to ask you. Tell you, I suppose. Before you go in there. That is. You should know it."

Since when did the Goblin King stammer? Freya looked over at him, bemused and wondering why now was the most important time to tell her anything. But then her stomach sank as she saw the expression on his face.

He was nervous. Anxiety nearly swallowed him up, and she couldn't imagine what he had to tell her that would make him so uncomfortable. He knew that she loved him, and he knew that she wouldn't fall under the Summer Lord's spell because she hadn't before with him. So why was he nervous now? Of all times?

"Eldridge?" she stepped closer to him and touched her hand to his cheek. "What's wrong?"

"Ah." He shook his head and forced a smile. "I've made you nervous, too. That wasn't why I wanted to talk with you."

"I always have time to talk about what you're feeling. Out with it."

He shook his head again, but at least cupped her hand with his own. Holding her against his cheek and inhaling as though he could smell her scent on the inner part of her wrist. "Just be careful. That's all I wanted to say. I know the Summer Lord is a handsome faerie, but he's no good."

She rolled her eyes and drew away. "That's what you're worried about? There's only room for one handsome faerie in my life. I couldn't handle two of you at the same time."

"No, of course not." He squared his shoulders and all the nerves fell away underneath the mask he wore. Not a real one made of metal or gemstones. The Goblin King's mask was one of flesh and years of experience. If he didn't want anyone to know what he was thinking, then no one would.

Freya could only hope she was so talented at hiding her emotions someday.

Together, they strode out of the castle and followed a white sand path. It was covered with tiny seashells that crunched beneath her feet. Not a cloud darkened the sky, and she knew this wonderful feeling wouldn't stay for long.

They followed the path all the way to a smaller garden, though still as lush as the others. This jungle setting was the perfect place for the Summer Lord and his veritable army of elves that draped themselves at his feet. A giant marble fountain sat in the center of the small pavilion. Two elves were seated on the edge, delicately sprinkling bits of bread into the water. Freya peered into the azure depths and saw bright orange koi fish swimming lazily to get their food.

She understood why the elves were so in love with this place. It oozed beauty and brilliance, but she also understood why the trees were mad.

There was a time and place for relaxation. Then there were times for action and purpose. What were these elves doing to better the world around them? Other than lazing about all day and indulging in their every whim?

The Summer Lord sat on a large couch they had brought into the jungle. Two elves fanned him with giant leaves.

He looked different from what she had grown used to. He had favored suits previously, just like Eldridge, who stood beside her in his classic black velvet suit with the gold embroidered edges.

The Summer Lord wore nothing more than white linen pants. The billowing fabric cinched tight to his waist. He wore many long loops of gold necklaces over his bare chest. Sweat slicked his skin and gave the dark color a sheen like oil. Rainbows danced over his chest every time he moved.

He lazily turned his gaze toward them and smiled, bright white teeth brilliant in the sun. "Ah, look who it is! The lovebirds I said weren't allowed to leave their cage. How do you two keep escaping?"

Eldridge bristled at her side. She knew he was about to argue, and that was the exact opposite of their plan.

She cleared her throat and stepped in front of him, purposefully twisting her body so the Summer Lord was looking at what she hoped was her best angle. "My Lord. You can't expect us to stay cooped up in the same room for days upon end while we're here. The Summer Court should be explored, don't you think?"

The words were supposed to make him think of all the lovely areas of his court. Freya had hoped he would wax on about the things that he loved. Eldridge certainly would have.

But the Summer Lord wasn't like the Goblin King. Instead of talking about all the things he loved, Leo narrowed his eyes at her. "What's that supposed to mean, little dove? You haven't fallen in love with this court, that would be a lie. If you're interested in Eldridge over here, then you would hate every aspect of my kingdom. Right down to every tiny seashell on my beaches."

At least Eldridge had calmed down enough to sound jovial when he responded. "You know that isn't true, Leo. I used to enjoy every summer that I spent here with you, and you remember that as well as I. Just because I haven't visited in a while doesn't mean I don't want to show Freya all our usual spots."

Leo's suspicious gaze turned to the Goblin King. "Usual spots? You hated every single one of them. I remember how often you used to complain here. It's too hot. It's too sticky. How could anyone live here when they could see the vibrant reds and oranges of the Autumn Court?"

Freya had worried the conversation would turn ugly. The two of them were incapable of being close to each other without a shouting match. If only she could get them to talk like civil men.

Once again, she stepped in between them and tried striking a pose. "Perhaps you would share your refreshments with me, my Lord? I quite enjoy being here and I remember the last time I met you, you had a wealth of delicious drinks."

Wrong thing to bring up.

Leo's cheeks darkened, and he sat up from his reclined position. "The last time you were here, you stole a very valuable magical item from me."

Oh no. Yes, she had stolen something from the Summer Lord, and she'd been trying to avoid that fact. Stealing wasn't something that the fae were particularly fond of, and most of the court leaders would have something to say to her.

She cleared her throat aggressively. "And I'm very sorry for that."

"I'd like it back."

Could this get any worse? Freya didn't have the little vial, at least, not with her. She assumed it was still in her things somewhere at the Goblin Court, but the vial with a lavender sprig in it hadn't exactly been her primary focus while traveling here.

She looked at Eldridge for his support, but he wasn't even looking at her. He was still glaring at his childhood friend as though his eyes could bore holes in the Summer Lord's shoulders.

Right, so she'd have to answer to the Lord on her own.

"I don't have it with me," she started, slowly saying each word. If she wasn't speaking quickly, maybe he would forget that they were trying to trick him. "But I'm happy to go get it later. I'm afraid I didn't realize how important it was to you."

"It's the only thing that keeps me calm." He gestured for one of the elves, and the lovely lady with the mask of a cat brought over a full goblet to him. "And no. You aren't getting any of my drink while you're here. The last time you drank me under the table, and the more I think about it, the less likely I believe it to be possible that you actually did that."

Maybe this was the game she had to play. If she revealed her tricks, perhaps he would be more inclined to speak with her.

Freya took another step closer and nodded. "I lied. I'm sorry for that, too. But I needed the vial to beat Eldridge and then discovered I like nothing more than doing that."

"Doing what?" Wine sloshed over his hand as he wildly swung the goblet around. "Lying?"

She rolled her eyes. "No. I don't enjoy lying, and I don't like to trick people as I did you. That's a faerie's game, not a mortal's."

"Exactly." The Summer Lord leaned forward, weaving slightly to the side before he gave her a half grin. "And yet here you are, with a faerie, lying through your teeth. How strange to think that you've learned your tricks from the Goblin King, while still being able to lie. You're a dangerous little creature, aren't you?"

Even like this, Freya was struck by how handsome this man was. In his suits, he looked stuffy and broad. But without the tight expectations of being the Summer Lord wrapped around his neck, he was a lean man with a crooked smile that lifted at the ends into dimples. He looked like the kind of man she'd find down an alley, ready to sell her dark magic spells for the cost of her soul. And she'd sell that soul to him, without question. A man like this could charm her into doing anything.

Well, almost anything. The thought of the Goblin King

would prevent her from doing too much more than selling him a soul. But it was still enough to be frightening.

"I don't want to lie or deceive you today," she replied.

"I don't think you know how to not do that. Why should I ever trust you?" He leaned back in his chair, that crooked smile still locked on his face. "Freya. You want something from me. Why else would you be here? That puts me in a position of power, and I think you've realized how little you want to do that. Because if I'm the one making all the decisions, then I will never make them in your favor."

"Then get us out of your hair." Freya quickly pulled back the bow string of her words and loosed an arrow she knew he would bite on. "We want to travel to the isles. Now I know you won't give us permission to do that, but at the very least you should consider it. Then we won't even be here. We'll be all those waves away from you."

At her words, his skin turned ashen and his eyes widened in fear. The goblet dropped from his hands, slipping to the floor and spilling red wine across the ground like blood. "You will never go to the isles. No one goes to the isles."

So something there was important to him.

Considering the way his hands shook uncontrollably, she would assume there was something on that island that could destroy him. Now, she very much wanted to go.

"I'll trade that vial back to you," she said. "All I want to know is how to get out there. That's all."

"On the back of a sea serpent," the Summer Lord snarled.

Eldridge put his hand on her shoulders and tugged her away from Leo and his elves. "Freya, we're not going to get his permission. I knew better than to ask this fool if we could have an afternoon away from all this."

She stared up at him with a frown. Freya was certain she was getting somewhere! All she needed was a couple more minutes and then she'd have him. Sure, she might be brow beating him into giving them permission, but she would have gotten what they wanted.

"Eldridge," she argued, but he put his finger on her lips. Silencing her.

The spark in his eyes was one of mischief. The Goblin King had a plan. She snapped her jaw shut and nodded ever so slightly.

"Be sad or angry," he muttered out of the corner of his mouth.

There was only one emotion that she could be convincing enough to act. Sad simply wasn't in her ability to fake.

Freya slapped her hand to his chest and shoved, hard. "Let go of me. I wanted to get out of here for a little while, and you promised you would see if you could make that happen."

Eldridge drew her farther away as he answered, "And I tried! I brought you to the Summer Lord, we talked with him, and he won't give us permission."

"You didn't even try to speak with him! All you wanted to do was argue!" She would have slapped him if she could bring herself to do it, but that felt too far. Besides, leaving a mark on his perfect face was more than a little wrong. She'd never forgive herself for it.

Soon, they were out of the Summer Lord's sight and nothing had changed. Freya looked around them, expecting something to happen and yet... nothing.

"Why did you want me to make a scene?" she asked, drawing away from him while crossing her arms over her chest.

He pressed a finger to his lips and grinned. "Wait for it. Scold me a little more, your shrewish voice is amazing."

"Shrewish!" she shouted, then immediately quieted down when he gestured with his hands. "I don't understand why we can't have private time together, that's all. I feel like the walls have ears here, and I wanted to get away. Just you and me."

The bushes rattled behind them. Freya lifted a brow and Eldridge mirrored her action, then waved a hand in the air for her to continue.

"I—I—" She decided to go for it. If they were supposed to be acting like they were in a fight, then she'd really sell it. "If we don't get some time together alone, then I don't see why we're even continuing this charade together. I'm done, Eldridge. Done."

An elf burst out of the greenery. "Wait! My lady, please wait. Don't say any words you can't take back until you listen to me."

Apparently, Eldridge had been right. They were being listened to and somehow their fight had swayed one of the elves. She put her back to the elf and mouthed, "Bravo," at Eldridge, before turning back around.

"What?" she grumbled. "I don't think you could say anything that would change my mind."

This elf was smaller than the others. Her delicate hands fluttered like birds at her side, and the butterfly mask on her face shuddered with the strength of her emotions. "You're such a lovely couple. I would hate to see the Summer Lord's cruelty ruin the beauty between the two of you."

Eldridge must have sensed weakness in this little elf, when Freya had been focusing on the Lord. Interesting.

She looked at Eldridge, then back to the elf. "That doesn't change the fact that I'm stifled here. I cannot be alone with him, and without that time, I will not be able to love him as before."

"Then go to the isles!" The elf stepped even closer to them, lowering her voice to a mere whisper. "There is a cavern down the beach. You can't miss it. Enchanted boats wait within and they will take you to the isles themselves. The Lord doesn't like anyone knowing they're there. But I know."

Freya reached out and patted the elf's shoulder. "You may have saved our relationship, my dear. Thank you."

The elf's gaze fell to the ground, and Freya was certain there was a blush underneath that mask. "It's my honor, Lady Freya."

She waited until the elf disappeared into the bushes again before turning to Eldridge with a shrug. "Well played, Goblin King. Well played."

He dusted his knuckles off on his jacket. "I've had a few centuries of trickery to learn how to manage these people."

"Apparently so. Shall we gather up Arrow and see what is on those isles?" She held out her arm for him to take.

"We shall."

CHAPTER 11

Freya watched as Arrow picked his way over the sands.
Every now and then he would stop, stare at the sticky
grains on his foot, and then shudder. He had forgone
clothing this time, certain the salt would destroy his precious
and luxurious fabrics. Freya and Eldridge had chosen matching
brown linen pants and white shirts that should keep them cool
in the hot sun.

Thankfully, Arrow wasn't complaining. The goblin dog was
more likely to do that than breathe, so she was automatically
suspicious. Even Eldridge was quiet when he should have been
waxing on about wherever they were going.

The cave appeared on the horizon, plunging into the white
cliffs and erupting with shadows that stretched out onto the
sands. Both Eldridge and Arrow stiffened at the sight.

Freya planted her hands on her hips and stopped walking. "All
right then, spit it out. You two know something I don't know."

They froze, each looking over their shoulder at her with a
guilty expression that would have rivaled her sister's when she
was a child. They thought they could wander through this place
without her noticing their fear?

Men.

Freya stomped toward them and pointed severely. "You two are worried about something. Why wouldn't you warn me we were going into a dangerous place? Here I was thinking it was just a cave, and instead, you're both planning for a fight!"

If either of them looked at the other one more time for information, she was going to explode. Freya crossed her arms over her chest and glared. They had no right to keep her in the dark on anything.

"Fine," Eldridge muttered. "I'll be the one to tell her. You owe me one."

"I'm aware," Arrow replied before trotting off into the distance.

Freya waited until Eldridge broke. She would say nothing until he gave her the entire truth. He owed her that much.

"Look, neither of us are certain there will be any danger in there. The Summer Court is relatively safe, but we're both worried that there might be some creatures in that cave that Leo has placed to keep people away from the boats. That's all." He held his hands up in a peace offering. "Since we weren't sure if there were actually going to be creatures, we thought it was smarter to not worry you."

"I completely disagree."

He rubbed the back of his neck and gave her a sheepish grin. "I thought you might say that. Look, I understand your hesitation and that you disagree with me. But can we go into that cave with our wits about us? We can always argue later."

She stomped past him, shaking her head in disapproval. "We could have walked into a trap and I'd be clueless."

"I didn't want to worry you!" he called after her.

Right. Or he didn't want to be wrong and then look like an idiot when nothing happened. Or when something actually happened, being embarrassed that he hadn't made a big enough deal about it in the first place. She should strangle him. It would save her trouble in the future.

She'd go in on her own if they insisted on being so ridiculous.

Without the two of them, she could focus on taking care of herself. Obviously she had to do that on her own, even though the two of them were supposed to be her dearest and closest friends.

Freya supposed they still were, even if they were a little ridiculous in their methods of taking care of her.

Sighing, she strode to the mouth of the cave where she waited for the two men to catch up to her. Sunblind, she stared into the darkness until it undulated like it had a life of its own.

Freya was used to that happening. The Goblin King's magic had prepared her to not be scared when the darkness moved. However, she was quite sure that the darkness wasn't expected to move in this case. Better to be safe than sorry.

By the time Eldridge caught up to her, Freya's eyes had adjusted. Large stalactites hung from the ceiling and dripped water down onto the stone floor. There was an impressive stairwell leading to a hidden place where the sea snuck underneath the cliff's edge. The water glowed bright blue with life.

How was this supposed to be scary?

She pursed her lips and waited for Eldridge to look over everything before she decided it was time to rub his fears in. "It's really terrifying," she said as she made her way down the steps. "I never would have thought you would be right, but look at all the terrifying creatures just waiting to take a bite out of us."

He watched her with a grin, letting her get her jabs in. Until he pointed to her right. "Like that creature, you mean?"

Freya turned and saw a giant crab latched onto the wall. Its legs were as long as her arms and spines grew on the sides of its shell. Tiny arms next to its mouth were working hard, picking at something it held clutched in its arms. It shifted, and she realized it was devouring a large meat rabbit that looked so small in the crab's grasp.

Fear zinged like electricity down her arms and she gasped, falling backward. She would have fallen to the ground if Eldridge hadn't caught her by the waist. "Careful," he muttered, staring behind her. "Apparently there's more of them than I thought."

She looked over her shoulder and a scream caught in her throat. There was yet another, this one standing on its legs, waiting for her to fall into its outstretched claws. The crab was four feet tall and could tear her apart if she slipped into its clutches.

Arrow carefully stepped next to them, his lips curled in a snarl. "I hate these things. Terrible monsters. Keep on the path you two, I suspect it's been spelled to protect anyone on it."

"Why would anyone ever step off this path?" she muttered.

"For those." Arrow pointed at the wall.

Gemstones were encrusted within the stone. Thousands of them, and likely worth a king's ransom. Rubies. Emeralds. Even clear chipped diamonds that should never have been able to grow where these were. And yet, here they were.

"Ah." Freya muttered. "Yes, I suspect many people would be enamored with those."

Eldridge squeezed her waist a little tighter. "Thieves fall under the spell of riches. Unfortunately for them, these guards are all too happy to pick them apart should they try to steal from the Summer Lord."

Suddenly, she was very grateful he'd asked her to steal off the Summer Lord's neck and not something down here. Freya wasn't so sure she'd have succeeded if he'd wanted her to bring him a gemstone.

They walked through the lines of crab sentries, and Freya tried her best to not anger them even further. By the time they all reached the boats at the bottom of the stairwell, the crabs were clacking their claws angrily. Each one she swore was glaring, threatening the intruders with the sharp edges of their claws.

Steadying herself with a hand on her hip, she looked at the first boat and pointed to it. "I think the one with a sun painted on it looks like good luck. What do you think, boys?"

Eldridge didn't even respond. He clambered into the wooden

vessel and held out his hand to assist her in as well. "I'm not sure we have a lot of time before the spell wears off and those crabs attack. I'd rather be rowing away when that happens, rather than standing here."

She hopped into the boat. He didn't have to argue with her about that any farther, and Arrow was quick to leap at her heels. Together, they pushed the boat away from the small dock and out into the glowing waters of the sea.

Eldridge settled himself on the bench where twin ores were notched in the side. He set his hands on them and they flew out of the cave. The opening to the sea was so low they all had to flatten themselves into the body of the small craft, but then the sun struck their faces with a wave of heat that slicked her skin with sweat.

But, oh, the sun was beautiful.

After the nightmarish creatures that lived in that cave, the sight of a cloudless sky was more than welcome. She leaned against the boat's side and stared down into the crystal clear waters. Tiny shells dotted the sand. Starfish the size of her head drifted across the ocean floor, while brightly colored fish flashed their scales and swam by.

This was the Summer Court she had expected to see. The entire ocean came alive with color and vibrancy that she'd never seen in her life. Compared to the other courts, this one was a veritable wealth of luxury for her eyes. She felt blessed to see any of the creatures here.

Except, of course, those horrible crab things.

Shuddering with the memory, she leaned back into the boat and eyed her companions. "How many other faerie creatures like that are there?"

"Plenty." Eldridge's shoulders flexed as he rowed, his arms moving them through the water with powerful strokes. "Wait until we get out into the open sea. I'm sure there are more creatures like that before we reach the isles."

She hoped not. Freya didn't want this feeling to be ruined by yet another monster.

Thankfully, they had time before any monsters attacked them again. The sun teased her face with warm kisses. Eldridge removed his shirt so he could row faster and easier. The glistening silver tones of his skin made him even more otherworldly, but still handsome. She'd never seen someone quite so inhuman, but still so tempting.

She wanted to lick every drop of sweat off his chest.

Arrow grumbled and turned away from her. "I can't stand it when you look at him like that. He's not a meal, you know."

"He kind of is." Freya lifted a brow and watched as Eldridge's cheeks darkened. "Wouldn't you say, Eldridge? Nothing wrong with making a meal out of a man."

"I'm trying to focus, love." Though his tones were scolding, his eyes burned with passion. "We'll take up this conversation again soon, but let me get us to the isles. Then we'll embarrass Arrow even more."

"I'm certain he doesn't mind." Freya had no intention of continuing the conversation, but teasing Arrow was too much fun. "We could continue in whatever way we want."

"Do you think?" He eyed Arrow as well, clearly understanding that she wanted to poke fun at their small companion. "I'm happy to go over the details of our nights together, however, I think the goblin is turning a little green."

Arrow burped, and the sound was horribly wet. "I don't do well on boats."

"Is that so?" Freya lifted a brow. "How interesting. And yet you do so well on carts."

"Not really." Arrow lunged for the side of the boat and threw up into the water. His retching echoed across the waves so loudly she was certain he could be heard from land.

Oh, the poor dear. Freya stopped teasing him and rubbed his back. "It's all right. I can see the isles! We can't be that far away from them. You'll make it."

Eldridge made eye contact with her and shook his head. Apparently the distance was more than she realized. Freya hadn't been on the water since she was a little girl, though, so she knew very little about their journey. Her father used to row her around a lake, but that wasn't the same as the sea.

The waters darkened as they grew deeper. Freya watched the waves get larger and felt her own stomach flip as they continued through foaming swells. Not once did Eldridge hesitate. His arms flexed. His back worked hard. And they didn't stop even when the waves were concerningly large.

"Eldridge?" she asked, yelling so he could hear her over the crashing water. "Should I be worried, yet?"

"Yes!" he shouted back. "Definitely worry!"

Well, that wasn't very reassuring. The boat they were in was small and the waves were large. She feared they were going to tip over, and Arrow wasn't helping the situation. He kept leaning over the edge of the boat, tilting them dangerously close to the water. His retching couldn't be controlled, but she also didn't want him toppling into the waves. Freya wasn't confident they'd ever get him back.

"Arrow," she said, exasperated. "Get back into the boat."

"I can't!" he moaned. "I can't stop throwing up and I'm afraid what will happen if I'm not near the edge!"

"Oh, you'll be fine." Freya picked him up and set him down on the floor of the boat. "Throw up on the floorboards, no one will mind. It's a boat. We can wash it."

"But then I can't see the isles!" He stayed where she put him though, dramatically moaning and holding his head between his paws.

If they could still see the isles, then she would have let him look. But Freya stared up at the waves and realized she had no idea where they were going anymore. The walls of water were so tall, all she could see was the darkness and foam.

The next wave swelled and a flash of teeth came with it. The shadow of the monster was larger than their boat. A sharp tipped fin and angular features warned Freya that this might be a shark. But she'd never seen one so big.

"Eldridge?" she called out again. "Please tell me you saw that!"

"I did," he said with a grim expression on his face. Eldridge released his hold on the oars and let the boat guide itself. "The best we can do is ignore the monster and hope for the best."

Right, ignore the giant shark that was in every single wave they rode over. She gulped and looked down, only to make eye contact with a black, soulless gaze.

Two sharks. There were more of the monsters. Lovely.

Freya reached for Eldridge's hand and gripped it tightly in her own. "If you aren't rowing the boat, how are we going to get to the isles?"

"I was never really rowing it." He lifted her hand and pressed a kiss to her knuckles. "It's magic. It'll take us to the isles no matter what. I just wanted to impress you in case things went poorly."

Somehow, even with fear turning her stomach, Eldridge made her laugh. Freya chuckled and pulled him closer, pressing a swift kiss to his lips. "Why? So I could see your bare, sweaty chest?"

"You enjoyed it."

"I did." Her heart swelled with the next wave and for a moment, she felt like she wanted to say "I love you".

Freya opened her mouth to let the words fall from her lips, but never had the chance. Eldridge put his hand on top of her head and shoved her into the deep belly of the ship. Flashing teeth snagged a few strands of her hair, and then the shark sank back into the waves without its prize.

"That was a close one," she whispered.

"Let's stay low until the ship makes it, shall we?" He sank down with her and pulled her against his heart. "We'll make it, Freya. I'm certain of that."

She wasn't, but Freya was glad he had faith. She didn't know how long it took for them to reach their destination. All she could focus on was the horrible sound of gnashing teeth scraping the bow of their boat and the splash of sharp tails striking the surrounding waves.

But eventually, their boat bumped against something that wasn't a shark's flesh. It was sand.

Freya was the first to look up and there was the isle. Right in front of her. They'd reached the singular point they needed to go to. And they'd made it alive.

CHAPTER 12

She staggered out of the boat and landed feet first in the clear, salty water. Gone were the raging waves and the cloudy sky overhead. This island was an oasis of beauty, peace, and lovely bird song. A small slope led up to the grassy area of the island that disappeared into a forest of lush trees and a brightly colored rainforest.

It was very similar to being on the mainland in the Summer Court. No sharks. No crabs. Nothing to deter anyone who had made it to the island.

Eldridge hit the sand beside her, tilting his head back and breathing in the clean, fresh air.

Poor Arrow wasn't doing well at all. He shambled on all fours toward the sand, threw up one last time, then buried his face in the cool water. A few bubbles erupted from his nose before he finally lifted his face with a gasping breath. "I can't do that ever again."

"I hate to break it to you, my friend, but we have to go back that way." Eldridge flopped his arms at his sides and chuckled. "There are no portals on the isles. We'll be back on that boat in no time."

Arrow groaned, then dramatically laid down in the sand. He

rolled onto his back, legs splayed in all directions, and then crossed his paws over his heart. "Then I will die here."

The dramatic goblin dog was exactly the relief she needed. Freya bent over, put her hands on her knees, and burst out laughing.

They had made it. They had traveled across that terrible ocean with all those sharks who had wanted to swallow them up. And they'd succeeded in getting to this damned island. Now, there better be a worthwhile secret that the Summer Lord was keeping from them or she was going to start breaking things.

When she caught her breath, Freya straightened and eyed the mysterious land. Where was the secret? What did she need to find that would be the thing the Summer Lord wanted to keep from them?

In one of the cliff edges she noticed there was a strange carving. The smoothed stone was a little too far for her to guess what it was. Squinting, she pointed over to the strange sight in the cliff. "What do you suppose that is?"

Eldridge looked the way she was pointing. He let out a little scoff. "Well. Would you look at that?"

"I can't," Arrow called out from his spot in the sand. "I'm dying."

"You are not," Freya scolded. "Eldridge, what are you seeing that I'm not?"

"I'm quite certain that's a house." He shaded his eyes from the sun, peering toward the strange carvings, but his eyes blurred. He stared as though he was looking into memories. "I had forgotten the Summer Court used to live in rooms like that. There were thousands of elves that lived all throughout the cliff faces, like pearls living inside clams. Why didn't I remember before now?"

She suspected it had something to do with magic. Why wouldn't it? Their entire lives had been molded, shaped by the ephemeral strangeness of powers that were beyond their control.

At least, sometimes. Unless one was the Goblin King, and then most magic was at his fingertips.

Shaking her head, she pushed for a little more information, wondering if he'd even remember such things. "Was there some kind of curse put on those who lived within the Summer Court?"

He shrugged. "I have no idea. But I'm curious to find out if there's someone within those walls who knows the answer."

Freya was just as curious. If the Summer Lord was hiding someone like that from the court, then he had a bigger secret than she imagined. What else had his powers hidden? Perhaps they were very close to what the forest wanted them to discover.

"Let's head into the house, then," she said with a bright smile. "One step forward, and an impressive one at that. Don't you think?"

Eldridge nodded, but his attention was still far from her reach. He walked across the sand toward the home like he was wandering through a dream. His eyes unfocused, his hair blowing in the wind. Sweat still glistened on his bare chest. Eldridge looked like some silver god of the sea who had strode out of the waves.

She would have followed him to the ends of the earth if he asked her to. And that terrified Freya to the very core.

They walked through the sands to the small home hidden in the side of the cliff. Or at least, Freya had thought it would be small until she saw how many small crevices opened up and disappeared into the stone. It seemed like there were hundreds of openings large enough for a grown man and woman to walk side by side through. The white stone cliff became a seashell with swirling secrets.

Eldridge peered into the first cave and braced an arm over his head on the stone. "I never thought to see a place like this again. Now that I can remember what happened when I was a child, the Summer Lord before Leo got rid of all these. He said they were dangerous."

"Why?"

He shrugged. "They aren't. No one could ever give a real reason for any danger. I suspect that the Summer Lord didn't like how easy it was for people to hide in them."

"Ominous," she muttered.

"It was." He stepped into the cave and disappeared from sight.

She didn't know if she should follow him or stay here. What if there were more crabs waiting for them? And this time there wouldn't be the added help of a spell keeping the creatures at bay.

Eldridge popped his head back into sight, glaring at her. "Are you coming or not? We have to see if there's anything in here for us to find."

Right. Of course they did. She wasn't supposed to be afraid when they'd just seen monstrous beasts from the depths of the sea that shouldn't exist.

Rolling her eyes, Freya walked through the small doorway and waited for her eyes to adjust. It didn't take very long, namely because the tunnel through the cliffs was very short. It took her ten steps and she was back in the sunlight.

Gleaming white rooms filled with light that spilled from holes in their roofs. Everything here had been painted with scenes from the ocean. Some murals were bright blue rolling waves, others were yellow like the sun. The room opened up to several others, creating a home out of carved spaces. She hadn't expected the inside of a cave to be so... welcoming.

Eldridge walked over to one of the small windows that looked into the other bright rooms and put his elbow on the edge. "Now I remember. So many elves used to live here, you know. So many."

"And they all left because one selfish man didn't want them here anymore." Freya shook her head. "That's a damned shame. I know many people who would be honored to live here. It's so beautiful."

Though there was a lived in nature to this home that felt

strange. If the elves weren't supposed to be here anymore, then why did it feel like the cups were too clean? The silverware had been laid out on the table as if someone was going to eat. And, strangely enough, it smelled like cinnamon.

Freya watched the area behind Eldridge, a small cozy room, and swore she saw the shadow of a person pass by. It stood to reason that they weren't alone, but she didn't know why anyone would hide. Unless they were afraid of the Summer Lord. Which, now that she thought about it, was entirely possible.

Strange, but not unexpected.

"Do you think this room is connected to others?" she asked, walking toward the other room and searching for the owner of the shadow. There was no one in the next space, but that didn't deter her. Freya knew in her gut there was someone to find.

"They all connect, yes." Eldridge looked around them. "Ah, there it is."

He touched his hand to a small glass knob on the wall that blended into the blue mural of the sea. The simple action very quickly opened a door she hadn't noticed that was perfectly painted into the blue coloring.

"Ah." Freya smiled and strode toward it. "So is this another room they would have used?"

"This would be their neighbor's home." He seemed to enjoy talking about the oddities of this place. "The elves aren't much for privacy, if you haven't guessed."

She'd assumed. Their homes were connected to the other families they lived near. She'd never wanted to be that close to the other people in her village. Freya was certain that would have driven her insane.

"Huh," she said, stepping into the other home. "How many homes do you think there are?"

Eldridge walked past her into the kitchen of this new home. This one was decorated with tiny daisies painted on the white walls. The oven was an ancient carved place in the wall, and now sunlight spilled through the chimney. He touched a hand to the carved name over the oven's opening. "Hundreds. More families than in the Summer Court now. There aren't as many elves as there used to be."

And what a horrible thing to think. All because one man had been so stubborn that he didn't want his elves to live here when they could live on the mainland with him. That sounded like her image of the Summer Lord. Including the current one.

Yet again, she saw a shadow streak by the white-washed wall. If there was a person here, then where were they hiding?

Maybe the person feared approaching such a large group. Freya had never been overly intimidated by one of the elves, so she couldn't imagine they were in any significant danger. Unlike the pixies, these were not a warring people. They were kind and shy, hiding their faces from the world because they worried about what would happen if they chose a face that someone else didn't like. The elves were not intimidating.

They were afraid, Freya realized. The elves were terrified of their Summer Lord, and that was why they wouldn't talk to her or her companions.

The last Summer Lord had taken them all from their homes, forced them to live where they didn't want. They had gone to the mainland when they were creatures of the sea.

Maybe the elves who currently lived on the mainland didn't remember their life here, just as Eldridge had forgotten. But she was sure they remembered deep in their soul their love of this place. And that they missed it more than they realized.

"Do you mind if I peek in this room?" she asked Eldridge. "I want to cover as much ground as we can."

"Do you think that wise?" Arrow sat down on her foot and stared up at her with disappointment. "Splitting up has only caused us trouble in the past."

"Splitting up saved us in the mines of the Spring Court, I'll remind you." She couldn't risk Arrow ruining her plan when the elf likely wanted someone to be alone so they could talk. "Why don't you go with Eldridge if you're so worried about being left behind?"

"He's right." Eldridge frowned, and she worried he'd already seen through her words. "If we split up in a place like this, we might never find each other again."

"We'll only go into a few rooms and then come right back here. Every room looks like it's painted differently, so I can't imagine they would be easy to forget." Freya flipped her hair over her shoulder and tried very hard to look like she knew what she was doing. "Besides, this is a ghost town in the wall of a cliff. There's no way anyone lives here. The Summer Lord made sure of it."

Eldridge hesitated, but eventually gave in. He grumbled something about headstrong women, but then scooped Arrow up under his arm. "Fine. I'll take the frightened dog. But don't go too far, and if anything happens—"

"I'll yell." She reached up and kissed his cheek. "You stay out of trouble too. I won't be there to save you this time."

"Ha. Ha. Very funny." He motioned that he was watching her before rounding the corner and heading into the next room on his side.

Perfect. Now her plan could work.

Freya darted into the next room and pitched her voice low. "I know you've been watching us. I saw your shadow a few times. It must be very scary to have three strangers walk onto your island after being on your own for so long."

There was no way to know if anyone was listening to her talk, but Freya was certain someone was watching her. The hairs on her arms were standing straight up.

She walked into the next room that looked like a bedroom. This one was painted with tiny elves dancing on every wall. The artist had spent many hours painstakingly perfecting each and every face. Even the dresses the elves wore swirled around them, appearing almost to move on their own even though they were painted.

Freya could stay in this room forever, but she had to find out who was in this abandoned place.

A gemstone had been stuck into the wall, held aloft by a painted elf who stood above the rest. She could only assume that was the button to get into the next room. Without thinking, she reached out and thumbed the small gemstone.

Well oiled and silent, the door to the next room swung open and revealed a garden waiting for Freya. The ground was covered in moss and tiny rivers that flowed to the center where a small pool held countless colorful fish. But Freya's eyes weren't on the greenery, the fish, or even the rivers that sloshed over her ankles. No, she was staring at the young woman crouched in the corner, staring at Freya with horror in her eyes.

She was beautiful with skin a deep umber. Her eyes were dark as midnight and glistened with unnatural light. Her hair was braided tight to her skull, individual strands standing out amongst the rest and nearly reaching her waist in length. Her clothing was old, outdated but still lovely, clinging to her strong, lean form.

But what shocked Freya the most was that this woman, this elf with her lovely pointed ears, had a face. She wasn't wearing a mask, but instead, she had a real face.

Just like the Summer Lord.

Freya stopped in the middle of the room and hunkered down on her haunches. "I'm not going to hurt you."

The woman's eyes only got wider. Clearly, she didn't believe Freya at all.

"Really, I'm not. I only came here to get some answers to questions that I cannot even begin to understand." Freya knew she was pushing this woman too fast and too far. But she had to try. "May I sit? I won't come any closer."

The woman shook her head, and Freya decided to take that as the other, not minding if she sat. The other option wasn't acceptable.

Obviously the woman didn't trust her at all. Her eyes flicked to a blank spot in the wall that could be a hidden door. Freya had to distract this stranger, or at least entertain her long enough to win her trust.

Shifting, she sat down onto the wet floor, crossed her legs, and sank her fingers into the watery moss. "Now. Let me tell you a story about a mortal woman who fell in love with the Goblin King. That'll help us get to know each other. What do you say?"

Fear was pushed aside by curiosity, and the woman relaxed against the wall. Freya took that as her opportunity, and so she began to tell her own story with all its strange and magnificent events.

CHAPTER 13

It didn't take long for Eldridge and Arrow to find them. Freya figured they'd only have a few moments alone, and she used those moments wisely. She spun a web of a story that would ensnare even the hardest of hearts. So by the time Eldridge walked into the room, she had already prepared the young woman to know who the Goblin King was.

Apparently, she didn't need to waste her time.

Eldridge walked through the door and his eyes grew wide. "Cora?" he asked. "What in the world are you doing here?"

To the other woman's credit, she didn't react at all to Eldridge's presence. "I should ask the same of you. You brought a mortal here and fell in love with her? That's not the Goblin King I remember."

He sheepishly rubbed the back of his neck. "I was a boy the last time we saw each other."

"Yes, you were. And you didn't yet know what it meant to be a king." The woman sighed and smiled at Freya, though the expression was sad. "I'm sorry I didn't speak. I thought you were lying. It's an incredible story you told and very few would believe the words true."

Freya shouldn't be so uncomfortable meeting someone

Eldridge used to know. She'd met countless others in the faerie realm, and yet this one unsettled her. Perhaps because the faerie woman was far more beautiful than the others.

Was this what jealousy felt like? Freya had tasted the emotion before, but only in small doses that hadn't felt like this. She could hardly think through the panic in her chest that warned she shouldn't let Cora and Eldridge anywhere near each other.

But that was silly. They were childhood friends, nothing more, nothing less.

"I wish you'd told me before my throat went raw," Freya replied with a small laugh. "But I'd like to know what you're doing here. Alone. Eldridge said this place was abandoned a long time ago."

"It was." Cora stood up and dusted off her sheer cream skirts. "Until the forest named me the sea. And after that, I was sent to live here by the Summer Lord. Far away from anyone else's gaze."

"The sea?" Those were strange words to use. The forest naming a person after the other element that made up summer? It sounded like what Cora had told them was important. But she couldn't make hide nor hair what it meant.

But even Eldridge appeared confused. His brows furrowed in concentration and he shook his head. "I think my mind's still foggy. I didn't remember what happened here until I stepped foot on the isles. I assume that's someone else's doing in wanting to hide whatever knowledge is kept here."

"The forest and the sea cannot live without each other," Cora said. She tucked her hands together in the picture of poise and delicacy. "The Summer Lord is no one without his lady, you see. So I've been here. Waiting for him to come to me so we can finally put the court back together. It's been a long time of being alone, but I know it's a matter of when he'll show up. Leo was always so late to everything that was important."

Freya's heart broke for this poor woman who was still holding out hope that Leo cared at all. In Freya's limited experience with the man, she wasn't so sure he was ready for a serious relationship. He seemed to hate himself a little too much to bring another person into his life.

She glanced over at Eldridge to see him staring at her with a thoughtful expression. "What?" Freya asked. "Why are you looking at me like that?"

Eldridge shook himself out of whatever thoughts had taken over. "Nothing. Cora, how long have you been here?"

"I don't know." She walked toward the small pool in the center of the room and sat down on the edge, swirling her legs in the water. "A while, I suppose? The last Summer Lord was the one who said I should stay here. And Leo was supposed to come get me when he took the mantle from the other. I didn't expect it to take this long, but I'm not surprised. The Lord was always a healthy man."

Oh, but it had been much longer than that. Did this poor woman not know how many years had passed since Leo became the Summer Lord?

"I—" Freya didn't know if she should be the one to tell this poor woman that she'd been here for a very long time. She wanted to go get the Summer Lord, drag him back to this isle, and force him to talk to Cora. Obviously, there were a lot of words left unsaid between the two of them.

If the Summer Lord was supposed to marry this woman, or unite with her, then this was the secret that Leo had been keeping. He wanted nothing to do with this picture of perfection, and Freya couldn't understand that. What man wouldn't want to be married to a woman like this?

She took a step toward the pool and crouched down once again beside Cora. "I think you've got the story mixed up, Cora."

The elf furrowed her brows and smiled at Freya with confusion in her eyes. "I'm sorry, I don't know how you'd know that? You're a mortal. The Summer Court's history has been hidden from your eyes."

"It's just that... Well. Leo has already taken the throne." She looked over her shoulder at Eldridge for some help. "It's been... How many years since he's been the Summer Lord?"

Eldridge's gaze darkened with anger and rage. "Nearly two hundred."

Cora's eyes widened with every word. Her feet stopped swirling in the pool and an unsettling quiet fell over the small garden hidden within the cliff.

What was going through this woman's head? Freya would have throttled Eldridge if she were in Cora's place. She would have put her hands around his neck and demanded to know why he had put not only their own relationship in peril but also the lives of so many others. The Summer Lord had a duty to take care of his court, and that duty was sitting right here.

Instead of doing any of that, Cora merely put a hand to her cheek and caught a single glistening tear that had slid from her dark eyes. "Oh." She looked down at the glittering droplet of saltwater and then smoothed it into her skin. "I suppose that means he doesn't want me."

"No!" Eldridge rushed forward and sat down on her other side. He reached for Cora's hands and gripped them in his own. "I remember you very well when we were children. Leo always tugged on your braids and chased you through the sands. He was very much interested in you, and I cannot imagine why he hasn't rushed to your side, even now."

"Because he doesn't want me." The smile on Cora's face was horribly sad. "It's all right, Eldridge. The forest picked us to be together, and I understand that's not always what the other person wants. I should be happy that I have lived my life out here, and not in the Summer Court while it collapsed without both of our attentions."

The two of them began speaking of their time as children. Eldridge reminded her of the small set of caves they had found that were filled with flowers no one had seen before. Cora giggled a memory of a grotto where mermaids lived, if only they waited long enough.

And suddenly, Freya felt as though she were intruding on private time between two friends. She stood up and made her way back to Arrow, who had laid down in a bright spot of sun.

She sat down next to him, beyond caring that the ground was wet. She had already soaked her bottom when she first came into the room.

"So they know each other, then," she murmured, pitching her voice low so she wouldn't interrupt the faeries at the pool.

Arrow snuffled and lifted his head from the soft moss. "Oh, yes. They were the best of friends back when the faerie courts liked each other. They spent every hour they could with each other until their parents wouldn't let them anymore. Sad stuff, that. Most people thought they would end up together."

Jealousy burned again. And she knew it was ridiculous to feel like that. People changed as their story changed, and the two faeries sitting next to each other were no longer the same children they had once been.

Still, it made her sick to her stomach to think she could lose him. "Is that so?" she gritted between her teeth.

"No." Arrow chuckled, sitting up so he could look at her better. "I wasn't even alive when they knew each other, Freya. You know when I was born. I imagine they were just good friends. Listen to the way she talks about Leo. Cora would do anything to have him in her life. She's in love with the fool."

It was hard to listen to the tones of love when she was so worried the other woman would take one look at the Goblin King and realize she'd picked the wrong friend. And maybe that was a ridiculous worry. She wasn't so caught up in her jealousy that she couldn't see that. But what if?

Again, Arrow made a snuffling sound and nudged her with his paw. "Freya. This look doesn't suit you. Jealousy is a poison as bad as what the forest is spreading through the Summer Court."

She sighed. He was right. Of course he was right when she was sitting here, green in the face, just because she didn't have the undivided attention of the Goblin King. Freya was acting like a child, and unlike herself when all she had ever wanted was to be an independent woman who took care of herself.

Shaking off the emotions with a quick jerk of her neck, she put her attention to fixing the problem laid out before them. The forest wanted the Summer Lord to do what needed to be done. And clearly, that was this woman in front of them.

Cora was the personification of the sea. And the Summer Lord represented the forest itself.

Frowning, Freya stood back up and interrupted the two of them as they continued talking about their childhood. "Cora? Might I ask a question?"

The beautiful woman looked over her shoulder and smiled. "Of course."

"The forest is punishing Leo for not joining with you, or whatever it was you said needed to happen. What happens to you if you don't become the Summer Lady?" Freya feared the answer would be just as bad as Leo's fate.

"Then the sea will take me back," Cora replied. "That's the way of the Summer Court."

The sharp edge of Eldridge's gaze bored into Freya's own. They couldn't let that happen. Neither she nor he were the kind of people who would let an innocent woman die without trying to save her. That was part of what made Freya fall in love with him so thoroughly. So dangerously.

Even with jealousy still bitter on her tongue, Freya hated to imagine Cora as the cold, still body she had seen so many times since coming to the faerie realm. This vibrant woman deserved to live, not die as the Summer Lord had resigned the both of them to.

"We won't let that happen," she replied. "Right, Eldridge?"

"We'll try to stop it," he corrected. "Leo is the only one who can save the both of you, and he isn't as you remember, Cora. Time has taken its toll on the Summer Lord."

Freya wanted to laugh, but she smothered the noise before it could burst free from her throat. Cora needed to remember Leo with all the possibilities of their future that she had been nursing for all these years. If this elf still thought there was a chance for her love to grow even stronger, then that made their task even easier.

"We'll need time to plan," she said. "I don't think we can go back to the Summer Court and demand that he come back here and take his bride home. Leo barely even speaks with us."

Eldridge stood and held out his hand for Freya to take. "We'll stay here for a few nights. I'm sure Arrow would appreciate the respite from all those horrible waves."

The goblin dog groaned from his corner and pressed a paw to his mouth. Apparently, the mere idea of waves made his stomach roll yet again.

Freya nodded. "All right. We'll stay for a little while and figure all this out."

CHAPTER 14

They tunneled deeper into the cliff until Eldridge found a room he thought was satisfactory. Freya noted how far that room was from where they had seen Cora, and where they had left Arrow.

The goblin dog was more than happy with the bright, sunny room painted with even more rays of sunlight. He'd laid down in a beam and said he was going to sleep until he forgot that adventure existed. Freya wasn't so sure why he had become so dramatic lately, but having a little time with the Goblin King to herself sounded like a good idea.

She wanted to kiss him. She wanted to run her hands over his shoulders and press her fingertips into him until he forgot all about Cora and her beauty. She still thought the jealousy was poisonous. Arrow was right in that.

But she couldn't shake free.

Eldridge chose a room that was darker than the others. It might have been the last room before they had stopped tunneling into the cliff. The walls were painted with deep blues and scenes from the depths of the ocean. Brightly colored squid with glowing tendrils. Fish with lanterns on their heads. And sometimes, if she looked closer at the dark paint at the bottom, she could see there were shadows of sharks added into the depths.

Beautiful and deadly. Just like her Goblin King.

He sat down on the edge of the bed and lifted his arms over his head with a yawn. "I am exhausted, aren't you?"

No. She wasn't exhausted in the slightest. She had a thousand questions running through her head and a million worries that he needed to ease. Why would he even think about sleeping at a time like this?

"We should talk about Cora," she said, approaching him with single-minded intent. "We should plan out everything that we intend to do. The Summer Lord won't be easy to convince that he should come back to the isles. Let alone that he should take a bride."

"I think we should get some rest and talk about it in the morning, when our minds are fresh." But his eyes glittered the closer she got to him.

Eldridge reached for her when she straddled his waist. Freya sat in his lap, wrapped her arms around his shoulders, and relaxed into the confident grip as he held her tight to his heart.

Maybe she didn't need to brand him with her touch. She didn't have to force him to be interested in her because of how many times she could pleasure his body. All she had to do was sit in his arms, listen to the beat of his heart, and shift her breathing to match his.

He rubbed her back with his hands, gently putting pressure on the tense muscles surrounding her spine. "You did good today," he murmured against her neck.

"Did I?" She pressed a kiss to his shoulder, inching a little closer as she did so. "I feel like I wasn't myself."

"Oh, because you turned green the moment you realized Cora and I knew each other?" he chuckled. "I saw how frustrated you were getting, my hero. Did you think I would miss that detail?"

Yes. She had thought he would miss her reaction to the two

of them. In fact, she had very much hoped he wouldn't notice at all.

Pulling back from his grip, she stared down at her hands. "I'm not proud of it. I know you're in love with me, and that you'd do anything to keep me in your life. There's no reason for me to be so jealous."

"No, there isn't." He reached up and brushed a strand of hair behind her ear. "But I know that this still feels very novel to you. As if our story is a fairytale you were sucked into, and someday it's going to spit you back out in your boring life by the forest. Isn't that right?"

To her great embarrassment, tears burned in her eyes. Freya refused to let them fall because crying right now would be utterly ridiculous. She had nothing to cry about.

So instead of letting her emotions get the better of her, she nodded.

"Oh, Freya." Eldridge stroked her jaw with a single finger, forcing her to look up at him. "I wish I could tell you in words how I burn for you. Every moment of every day I fall deeper in love with you. When you are at your worst and when you are at your best."

This man made her melt. He never failed to ease all her worries and remind her how much she loved him. And she wanted to say it. She wanted to tell him that her heart beat for him and that no matter where she was, she always thought of him.

But she couldn't. Not yet. Not when he knew how jealous she was of his relationship with Cora. If she said the words now, then he would think she was only saying them because there was the possible threat of another woman.

And that wasn't how she wanted him to remember this moment. She wanted Eldridge to know that without a doubt in her mind, she loved him. A thousand times more than there were stars in the sky. Regardless of old flames.

She settled back into his arms and let him draw her into the bed with him. Eldridge tucked her head into the crook of his shoulder with a happy sigh. "You and me, Freya. We're the same kind of creature, you know that? Adventurers at heart. We don't stay in the same place for very long, and I've always admired that about you."

What if she wanted to stay in the same place for a while, though? She hadn't been this person before she met him, and Freya worried he'd get bored with her.

Eldridge's breath evened out into the deep rhythm of sleep. But while the Goblin King found himself in the dreaming world, Freya couldn't even consider sleeping. Her mind was racing with all the things that she needed to get done. To think about. To understand.

Cora was the personification of the sea in this equation. And she could understand that there was a connection between the land and the sea. They were two elements who were constantly touching, but never existed in the same plane. They were the perfect symbols for magic to grow and develop.

What she didn't understand was how a person could be on an island by herself for over two hundred years and never realize how fast the time was passing. Freya would have been counting the days on the walls. Every room in this cliff side town would have been painted with tiny numbers as she waited for someone to come and get her. Wasn't that the same feeling Cora must have had?

Two hundred years alone was a very, very long time.

And then there was the reasoning why the Summer Lord didn't want to make her his Lady. After all, Cora seemed to be the perfect choice for such an illustrious position.

Mortals did this all the time. Nobles married people they weren't in love with, but who were good political matches. They made it work. She was certain they didn't exactly enjoy the company of each other. Most likely they focused on their own lives, and that was that. Why wouldn't the faeries do the same thing?

Rolling over in bed, she planned to ask Eldridge what made the faeries so different from the mortals. But he was sleeping. His features were smooth as glass, relaxed as she hadn't seen him in a very long time. She shouldn't wake him when he had fallen into a deep sleep.

Freya inched herself closer and closer to freedom. She tried very hard not to jostle the bed with her movements, and made it out of the covers, then to the very edge of the room. She spared a single glance back to look at her handsome Goblin King one more time.

"I really do love you," she whispered, letting the words float into the shadows and hopefully into his dreams. "And when the timing is perfect, I will tell you that with so much certainty that you will never question it again. My love. My life. My Goblin King."

Slipping out into the hall beyond, she weaved through all the homes of the neighborhood. Freya understood Eldridge's fear that she would get lost in the countless rooms and then no one would ever find her again. But she didn't share the same concern.

Each home was distinctly different, but there were markings. The elves had gotten in and out of these cliff side homes with ease, and that wasn't because they knew every single neighbor and where that neighbor lived. They had a pattern. A tool to getting out even while they marched through the living space of another.

She put her fingers to the frame of a door and thumbed the markings carved there. Three lines, each one distinct. One wavy, two straight but a little shorter than the other. Strange markings, but ones she was certain had to do with the direction to go in.

And she had all night to figure it out.

Freya strode through colorful rooms and made up stories in her head about the elves who used to live here. The ones who painted flowers on their walls missed living on the mainland, but they were happy here on the islands as well. The ones with dolphins were the funny family, the tricksters who always played pranks on their neighbors. Her favorite, though, were the ones who painted elves on their walls. Those were the artists she fell in love with. The elves who had stories to tell and didn't want to forget them no matter what.

Eventually, she figured out what the lines meant. The waves were directional, telling someone to go left or right depending on the direction of the pointed crests. And the other two lines were how far to go. The top line was the distance to the sea. The bottom was the distance to the end of the neighborhood.

In very little time, Freya stood on a balcony overlooking the sea. A full moon illuminated the white sand beach, and the stars were so bright, it looked like the sea sparkled with a thousand glowing fish. Perhaps this was how Cora had stayed here all these years and never once questioned how long it had been. With a sight like this every evening, Freya didn't think she'd want to leave either.

The shadows to her right shifted, and Cora appeared out of the darkness. This time, the lovely woman didn't speak at all. She watched Freya with hope in her eyes, and a sense of oddness that could only come from a someone who had spent very little time in the presence of others.

"You and Eldridge share that ability, you know." Freya smiled. "The two of you are always popping out of shadows and startling me."

"Oh." Cora looked behind her, and then a sheepish grin crossed her face. "I forget that mortals can't see very well in the dark. I thought you knew I was here."

She hadn't, and the excuse was a foolish one. Freya used this chance to get to know the other woman, however awkward that might be. The more she knew about Cora, the easier to convince the Summer Lord to come to the isles.

Freya leaned against the railing of the balcony and crossed her arms over her chest. "Why do you want to marry the Summer Lord?"

The elf's eyes widened in shock before she stammered, "Well... I... I..."

Yeah, Arrow was right. The woman was madly in love with the idiot, and Freya understood the fear that came with that realization. It was a bone deep need that never went away, no matter how hard they wanted to be their own person. Both Eldridge and Leo had wiggled into their very souls. The fiber of who they were.

Freya sighed and reached out to take the other woman's hand. "Is there a kitchen where we can talk? I think I'd like a cup of tea, if you have any."

"Oh, I have more than enough tea to satisfy both of us." Cora squeezed Freya's fingers with a radiant smile on her face. "Come on. We'll have a chat. I'm afraid it's been a very long time since I've had another woman to speak with."

Freya suspected that was very much the truth.

CHAPTER 15

The kitchen Cora brought her to was warm and inviting. A fire crackled in the oven that was inlaid into the wall, and the table was filled with dirty dishes, food, and countless other objects from the sea.

Freya picked up a dried starfish and held it aloft. "One of yours?"

"I like to collect things on my walks. Sometimes I find items from the mainland that people have set adrift." Cora reached for the starfish and gently set it back down on the table. "Other times, I find treasures that the sea sends me."

A treasure. Freya looked down at the small dead creature and supposed it was a bit like a treasure. Esther had once gone to the sea with Freya and their father. They had collected sand dollars to put in a jar, and Esther had loved looking at them.

"Treasure," she repeated with a soft smile. "That's a lovely way to look at it."

Cora spun around and grabbed for teacups that hung from tiny hooks on the wall. She set about putting a large metal teapot directly into the fire and then filled her arms with a mound of dirty dishes that likely should have been cleaned weeks ago. "Lovely is correct! Just don't look at my mess. I'm afraid living alone has made me... well."

Freya reached out and grabbed a plate before it fell out of Cora's arms. Though there were likely plenty of plates to steal from other homes, she suspected Cora liked these the best. "You've only had to take care of yourself and not had to worry about the opinions of others. I completely understand."

She'd get messy too if she didn't have to clean every single day. It was so much easier to let things be as they were.

"Exactly." Cora precariously took the dishes over to the corner where she laid them down into a box. "I usually wash them in the ocean, you see. I just haven't had time lately and..."

No more words came out to explain her predicament away. Freya grinned and lifted her teacup. "We have two clean teacups! That's all we need right now."

The expression on Cora's face brightened once again. "I like the way you think, Freya. You're a good friend, I can tell that already."

As Cora bustled about the kitchen, searching for tea, Freya suspected, she peered into the teacup. There was a giant stain on one side, and the other was still muddy with soot. At least, she hoped the black substance was soot. Making a disgusted face that she couldn't suppress, she picked at the black goo and pulled it off with her finger. Maybe that wasn't soot. It was a little too thick.

"Here we are!" Cora exclaimed.

Freya wiped her expression clean of any expression. "What kind of tea did you find?"

"It's only earl grey, but it's something. I hope you like strong tea?" Cora asked, then emptied the entire container into the teapot.

Freya could only hope there was a strainer in all that, or they would both be picking tea out of their teeth for weeks to come.

"I love strong tea." She gestured to the holes in the ceiling where sunlight would normally filter through. "Especially when it's nighttime. If I'm going to stay up all night, I might as well have a good cup of tea to help keep me awake. Don't you think?"

"I do." Cora sat down in the chair on the opposite side of the table and put her chin in both hands. "You wanted to know why I hope to marry the Summer Lord?"

Here they went, telling each other stories as women often did by candlelight. At least she'd get a few secrets out of this strange and messy ordeal. "I do. I know you haven't seen Leo in a very long time, but I can't imagine he's the same boy you remember."

"Probably not. But I'm not the same girl I was back then, either." Cora gestured around at the mess. "Believe it or not, I used to be very clean."

Freya snorted. "This mess doesn't come from a couple hundred years on your own. I don't think you ever were the tidy woman you describe yourself to be."

"No. But I did at least have servants to pick up after me." The elf shifted on her seat, obviously uncomfortable that the mess was so uncontained. "I just... Look. I remember Leo when he was a boy, and there was always an edge to him. He was a little dangerous, and someone that a girl like me would fall head over heels for. I always knew there was a level of uncertainty in our relationship. But I never questioned that we could and would get married."

"So you knew?" Freya moved the cup into her lap as though she wanted to hold it. Instead, she used the edge of her shirt to clean the interior. "You knew that you were going to get married to him, that is."

"We both could guess. The titles of Lord and Lady always goes to the strongest of the fae in the court. He and I were the obvious choices." Cora leapt up at the scream of the tea kettle. "I was much more interested in the possibility than Leo, as you must have guessed."

Freya assumed. She held out her cup and let the conversation fall silent as Cora poured the mixture of tea leaves and liquid into Freya's teacup. The silence wasn't awkward between them, though. It was simple and quiet. Like two friends who hadn't been able to talk together for a very long time.

Sipping carefully so she didn't get any leaves, Freya cleared her throat. "Can I ask you a question that might be rude, but I honestly don't know if it is?"

Cora grinned into her cup. "Those are my favorite kinds of questions. By all means. Ask away."

"Why do you and the Summer Lord have faces, but no one else in the Summer Court does?" Freya didn't know if that was overstepping her bounds. After all, the ownership of a face seemed like a very personal thing. Even if it was just a choice, she assumed that still meant it was personal.

"Oh." Cora laughed a little and set her cup down. "That's not so hard to answer. Surprisingly, the Lord and I picked our faces together when we were children. Usually an elf would take a long time to decide what face they wanted to commit to. Neither of us saw the reason for that. So we went to the mortal realm, tried on more faces than I can remember, and then we both settled on these."

They tried on mortal faces? Freya didn't like the sound of that, but her curiosity burned ever brighter. "Whose faces were they? Or do you not remember?"

"Of course I remember. A face is a thing that is freely given by mortals, even when they don't realize it. But they mean so much to the elves." Cora touched a finger to her cheek. "They were a young couple, very much in love and so looking forward to the rest of their lives together. I knew when I saw her face that she loved her husband more than the sun loves the moon. I had to have that expression when I looked at Leo on our wedding day."

Freya's heart melted. "What a lovely thing to desire. And Leo must have felt the same if he took her husband's face?"

"We thought it would be poetic. We'd tell the story to the other elves, they would all melt at the story of our young love, and the entire court would fall in love with our own story." She shrugged. "I guess it just wasn't meant to happen like that after all."

This poor woman shouldn't feel like she had done something wrong just because a man hadn't chosen her. The Summer Lord's adoration was no more impressive than that of a simple farmer's love, and Cora would have made a thousand people fall in love with her in the mortal realm.

She reached across the table and grabbed onto Cora's hand. "I don't think that anyone's love is lesser because of a choice they made. It sounds like the Summer Lord had intense feelings for you, and I don't know why he decided not to act on them. But before I leave this court, I promise you, I will try to find the answer for you."

Cora squeezed her fingers in return. "I don't know where you came from, or why you're helping me, but I can see why Eldridge loves you so dearly. Your heart is more pure than anyone I've ever met. The fae are not..."

"Like the mortals?" Freya grinned and shook her head. "I assure you, there are a million people in the mortal realm who are kinder and more giving than me."

She could list off a handful of priests who would be horrified to know that any faerie thought Freya was a good person. After all, she had been the one to skip mass more times than was acceptable. But the reality was that she was trying to be a good person, and perhaps that was where so many of the fae failed. They were selfish creatures by design. They expected other people to take care of them, but all the fae were like that. When there were a hundred takers, and only one giver, she could only guess that faerie would end up in the mortal realm.

Her grin nearly splitting her face, Freya leaned back and released her hold on Cora's hand. "If you weren't so dead set on winning Leo back, I'd tell you to run to the mortal realm. You might meet some fisherman who steals your heart and thinks being married to the sea would be the best thing that ever happened to him."

"Oh, I doubt that." Cora's cheeks darkened. She sipped at her tea and made a face. "This is horrible."

Freya sucked in a deep breath and nodded, gently nudging her tea away from her. "Yes, yes, it is quite bad. I think there was something in the cups that gave the tea a distinctly fishy flavor."

"I'm so sorry." The laughter in Cora's voice was everything that Freya needed to hear. The bubbling sound was so wonderful, so heartfelt, and it was the first time she'd heard Cora's happiness.

And that was all Freya wanted for this kind, sweet woman who had been locked away by everyone who mattered. She deserved to be happy, even if Freya had initially been jealous of her beauty.

"That's quite all right," Freya said with a chuckle. "Just don't make me drink it anymore, and I'll forgive what horrible tea making skills you have."

"I would not be a very good lady's maid."

"No, but I can't imagine the Lady of the Sea requires such a skill set. There are quite a few women who will be ready to wait on you when you return to the Summer Court." There had to still be people there who remembered Cora, like Eldridge had. And what a welcome surprise that would be.

At least, Freya hoped that was the welcome this wonderful young woman would get. Even though the Summer Lord hadn't wanted her as his bride, that didn't make Cora any less worthy. It wasn't like Leo was going to pick one of the other elves in his court. Freya didn't think he wanted to be married at all, and that was the problem here. Not that he didn't want Cora.

She hoped.

Heavens, she hoped that was the case because otherwise she and Eldridge had their work cut out for them.

Patting Cora's hand one last time, she stood up. "I should get back to the room where I left Eldridge. If he wakes up and I'm gone, I'll never hear the end of it."

Cora stood with her, a swift smile breaking out over her features at the mention of the Goblin King. "He'd like that. Knowing where you are when he wakes, that is. He's very protective of you. I could see that in the few moments we were all together."

That jealous knot in her stomach twisted yet again. And it shouldn't. She knew it shouldn't.

Cora was being kind. She wanted Freya to know that as a friend of Eldridge's, she could see how strong his reaction was when Freya was around. Yet, it was still hard to stomach that Cora could see what Freya still had a hard time seeing.

Giving the other woman one last smile, Freya nodded again and left the room. She hoped that in leaving, she wasn't giving the wrong impression.

She just couldn't stay a single minute more while her mind whispered a mortal would never be enough.

CHAPTER 16

Together, she and Eldridge pushed the boat back into the waves. The small vessel had done them well on the journey to the isle, although Freya wasn't looking forward to whatever waited for them in the deep seas again.

Cora stood on the beach, wringing her hands with worry marring her usually pretty expression. "Do come back!" she called out. "The sea won't make it difficult for you this time. Everyone wants the elves to be on the mainland. Even the ocean."

"We'll come back!" Eldridge called out. He deposited Arrow in the bottom of the ship. The poor dog already looked green in the face. "And next time, we'll bring Leo to see you!"

Freya smiled but couldn't stand to see the frantic waving of the lovely woman for a moment longer. She needed to get back to the mainland and center her mind before charging into Leo's room with a single-minded intent. The man would return with them to this isle and he would give Cora a chance. Even just to talk.

The entire court depended on it.

She clambered over the edge of the rocking boat and waited for Eldridge to slip in as well. Saltwater clung to her legs and a cold chill danced down her spine. Leaving Cora behind felt wrong, but the elf had made it very clear that she was to stay on the island. Even if she wanted to go with them.

Eldridge picked up the oars, and they were off. Flying through the sea surf as though the boat had wings.

"You don't have to row, you know," she said with a quirked brow.

"I know." He heaved back, the muscles of his biceps rippling. "Feels good to use my body, though. Wouldn't you agree?"

His waggling eyebrows suggested she should be warmed by the sight of him. But there was too much on Freya's mind to enjoy the look of her Goblin King. And he was hers, even when she was second guessing herself.

Sighing, she dropped her head into her hands and let out a long groan. "How are we going to get the Summer Lord to come back here? I think he's quite happy in his choice that he isn't interested in whatever Cora can offer him. In fact, I would argue to say he's going to banish us from this court entirely at the mere suggestion that he should return here."

The sound of oars striking water continued for a few moments before Eldridge replied. "We'll find a way. We always do. He'd be very lucky to have Cora at his side. And from what I remember when we were young, he was also very interested in having her. I don't know what changed."

Arrow nosed his way underneath her legs and stared up at her with big, brown eyes. "If there's one thing I know, it's romance. The Summer Lord is afraid of what a life with Cora might look like. And that kind of fear is normal, but we need to remind him that it doesn't have to be an awful life."

"And?" She wanted more than that. She knew the concept of love was terrifying to some, especially the idea of marriage. Even Freya hadn't wanted to consider herself shackled by a man.

Until now, she realized. If the Goblin King had wanted to spend his life with her, then she would say yes. But it would be a brief life for him, and Freya couldn't imagine why a faerie would ever tie himself to a mortal who could die at any moment.

Shaking herself out of such thoughts, she sat back up and stared out over the ocean. The shore was much closer than she expected, and the seas weren't quite so deep. Almost like they were traveling through an entirely different ocean. "I think we need more of a plan than simply talking about Cora."

"I think talking about Cora is the first step." Eldridge set the oars down and braced his arms on his knees. "He has to remember her. The feelings she inspired in him. How wonderful being in her presence made him feel. All of those things are the first steps toward convincing him to at least see her."

She had a feeling he was speaking from experience. That at the sight of the person he loved, the Goblin King could only think of the good memories. She hoped, at least.

Freya nodded and tried to release some of the tension in her shoulders. "We'll run with that. I hope he understands and wants to see her. He's a good man. She's a good woman. They would make a suitable match."

As Eldridge turned his attention back to the mainland, Arrow touched his cold nose to Freya's hand. She glanced down at him to see worry reflected in his eyes.

"It's just..." Arrow pitched his voice so low, she almost didn't hear him. "What if he doesn't want her because she was picked for him? What if he wanted to choose for himself?"

"Then that's a hurdle we'll have to overcome when we see him." Freya feared the same thing. The Summer Lord could dig his heels in for any reason, and they had to be prepared for any reaction.

Before she knew it, they hit the mainland. The boat rocked gently, not a single monstrous creature having disturbed them, and she was shocked to realize that this journey had been easy.

Turning around, she stared back toward the isle where she could see dark storm clouds gathering. It was impossible that they had traveled without touching that storm, or those horrible sharks that had wanted nothing more than to chomp through their flesh. But they had journeyed with no issues back to the mainland. Likely their next visit to Cora wouldn't be so easy.

Frowning, she left the boat and stood in the sands, waiting for her companions to join her.

Eldridge already scowled, staring up at the castle of the Summer Lord with anger in his eyes. "This will be an argument unlike any I've ever had before."

"Most likely."

He shook his head. "I'm going to see what I can find around the castle that might help us."

"Oh." Freya had hoped they might have a few moments together before they started this insane plan. She wanted to reconnect with him, to breathe in the air of his lungs, so she could be sure that none of what was in her head was real.

But she hadn't asked for that, and now he already had another plan. She knew he was right, as well. They would need more than a memory to convince the Summer Lord to go to the isles with them. And even though that memory would be a major part of their plan, they might need a few additional tricks up their sleeves.

Not a single thought trickled from her mind to her tongue. Instead, Freya nodded and took a step away from him, down the beach and toward the caves where they had first searched. "I understand. I'll do the same."

He looked over at her with a frown. "Shouldn't you search through the castle, too?"

She tried a bright smile, but feared it wasn't very convincing. "I'm going to start on the beaches. It's where it all started, didn't it? There has to be something, or someone, I can find down here."

Though obviously suspicious, Eldridge didn't argue with her. He made his way up the beach toward the stairs that would lead him to the castle. Arrow tottered off after him with a sickly smile and a quick, "I'm going to clean myself up."

Why couldn't it be easier? This relationship between herself and the Goblin King? Freya wanted to let go and love this faerie man who so dearly wanted to wrap her up in his love. The warmth of his affection should have been enough for the fear in her chest to dissipate. And yet, it wasn't.

A deep hum in the earth beckoned her toward a small crack in the cliff's wall. Just large enough for a woman like her to fit through. Eldridge would never have managed to follow her. She already knew who wanted to speak with her.

Freya didn't argue or hesitate. She squeezed through the crack and emerged into the emerald forest beyond. The trees swayed at her presence, their branches leaning down to touch her hair and her shoulders.

They didn't speak this time. The dead things in their roots didn't move. She was allowed to walk all the way to the largest tree in the forest where the man with vivid green eyes waited for her. He opened his arms, gesturing for her to enter the grotto without hesitation. "So you found her."

"I did," she breathed. "I think Cora is an excellent match for him, although I don't know why he would defy you in this."

"Simple," the tree replied. "He doesn't want to do anything we tell him to do."

"Sounds like a spoiled child." Freya remembered Esther going through the same phase. Freya would tell her to wash, and the answer was no. Eat. And again, the argument would continue. Whether she wanted something from Esther or not, the child would never do what Freya wanted because it was Freya who had asked.

The tree nodded the dead elf's head, expression wise and sage as an ancient being should be. "You understand. He is an exceptional boy, and we raised him well when he was first given to the forest. But faeries age a lot slower than mortals."

"Hundreds of years in the teenager stage." Freya shook her head and sighed. "I pity you."

"Pity." The man tilted his head back and burst into laughter.

"That's the first time anyone has ever said that to me. You are a refreshing distraction, my dear Freya."

She supposed no one was likely to pity someone like this. An all powerful being who used the dead to speak. She understood how her statement must have been a novelty.

But she really did feel for the tree. She knew what it was like to give and give, only to be certain that the person you're giving to would not appreciate all the work.

Freya wished she had more time to commiserate with this powerful being. It was making her feel better. However, she had to work on convincing the Summer Lord to do what the tree wanted, and that was going to take a very long time.

"You asked me to come here," she said. "What else do you need?"

The man shrugged, and the tree lit up with bright, golden lights that swirled around the base. "I didn't ask to see you, Freya. You wanted to come here. You wanted to see us, or perhaps there was someone else you desired to speak with."

"Speak?" Words stuck in her throat at the mere thought of speaking with her father. He had been gone for so long, she didn't know if she had anything to say to him. Would she get angry like she had her mother?

Freya still didn't know what to say to the woman who had raised her. Her mother was the one who was supposed to take care of both her and Esther, but her father? He was the flagstone that anchored their family down. And all of this was his fault. That damned werewolf should never have bitten him, but because it did, her entire life had turned upside down.

The man nodded toward the cage of roots. His eyes darkened with magic. "See for yourself. Magic can do a lot of good as well as a lot of harm, but you know that already."

Heart pounding, she stepped toward and peered into the shadows of the root prison.

The fur had almost entirely left her father's body. He sat in the back corner, as a man might sit. His head in his hands that were still lightly furred. But his feet were human. And the baggy pants that didn't quite fit his thighs weren't ripped. He was more a man than she had seen in a very long time.

"Father?" she whispered.

He looked up, and those eyes weren't his. Not yet. He was still a beast inside the body of a man. But the werewolf had recognized her, and this creature lifted his head, sniffed the air, and she knew the moment he realized that Freya was his daughter. His eyes brightened. His shoulders squared more as though the presence of his own family gave him strength.

Her bottom lip quivered. Her father was looking at her as he used to. With so much love and pride in his eyes, even though she knew this wasn't really her father. He was a beast in a man's body, but that didn't matter.

They were so close to saving him.

She reached out her hand, slipping it through the roots and waiting for him to approach. "Hi, Dad."

He stepped closer and reached out. His fingers were calloused and rough as he wrapped her hand in his. She remembered his hands feeling like this. Not a single day had passed when he wasn't working in the woods or using his hands to do something that would leave tiny cuts and scrapes all over him. Such hard labor had turned his grip into iron and his skin into leather.

Tears blurred her vision and she let out a little laugh, staring up at his face that was wrinkled with concern. "You grew a beard," she whispered with a small chuckle. "You look awful with a beard, you know. Mother always hated them."

He tilted his head to the side and frowned. "Daughter?"

"Yes." She nodded, not wanting to lose this moment and watch him trail back into those beastly ways. "I'm your daughter. Freya."

This time, there was even more recognition in his eyes. He looked at her as a father did a child, with a soft gaze and the knowledge that he had created someone who was the spitting image of himself. "Freya," he repeated. "Yes. That is your name."

She wished she could believe he remembered more than that, but Freya knew that was unlikely. He only knew of her as Freya and that she smelled like him. It was enough for now, because rushing the process of healing could take more of her father away from him. Memories took a long time to return.

Squeezing his fingers in hers, she pressed her forehead against the root bars. "I wish I could ask you how to get the Summer Lord to the isles. You always had the best ideas."

"Summer Lord?" The frown on his face deepened. "He fears the isles."

It was surprising that he knew. Perhaps she wasn't giving her father enough credit, even though it was still the wolf looking back at her. "Yes, I suppose he does fear the isles. There's a woman there who waits for him, and he doesn't want to see her."

"Ashamed."

She jerked her head back up and stared into her father's eyes. "What did you say?"

He released his hold on her hand and retreated into the shadows of his prison. "He's ashamed to see her. To let her see who he has become."

Freya wasn't so sure if her father was talking about himself, or if he was talking about the Summer Lord. She supposed the words were meaningful for both of them. If the Summer Lord knew that his drunken nature was an embarrassment, but couldn't stop, then why would he want to see Cora? He'd been the strong, handsome elf ready to take on the throne. Now, he was nothing more than a drunken fool who threw parties for a dying court.

Was he embarrassed to let the woman he loved see who he had become?

"You might be onto something, Dad," she whispered. "And it's a great place to start a conversation with the elusive Summer Lord."

CHAPTER 17

Freya emerged from the cave hours later, certain that she was on the right track. Though her father wasn't even close to human yet, he was making progress every single day. The trees were making good on their promise. Now, it was her turn to show that she had what it took to convince the Summer Lord to take up his rightful position.

She stepped into the sunlight, blinking away the sudden blindness from the white sand beach. She would never get used to the sun here. Everything was so bright and vivid, no matter which direction she looked.

But when she could see through the stars in her eyes, she noted a figure standing in the middle of the beach. A dark figure, outlined by the sun itself, staring out to sea as though there was something there waiting for him.

She supposed there was, although she would be surprised to hear that he cared.

The Summer Lord stood in loose pants made of silk and chiffon. They blew in a light breeze and the tails of the band at his waist whipped. His chest was bare other than a few symbols painted in bright gold. He was handsome in a way that was breathtaking sometimes.

She walked up to his side and was shocked to realize there wasn't even the hint of alcohol in the air. She didn't smell beer or wine or mead. Just the barest scent of lemongrass.

He was sober. She didn't think she'd ever seen him sober.

She mimicked his posture and tucked her hands behind her back as well. "Leo."

"Freya." He glanced down at her with a curled lip. "I don't like you using my name."

"You don't like me at all. So it wouldn't be the end of the world if I used your name. It's not going to change how you feel about me." She stared out to sea, even though she could feel him looking at her. "Besides, we have more to talk about than if you want me to use your given name or your title."

"More to talk about?" His voice betrayed not a single emotion, but he shuffled his feet in the sands like he was uncomfortable.

Freya had learned how to read the fae. She knew when they were trying to get around a subject that they didn't like. She knew when they felt like she had pushed too much. Leo was feeling all of these things and more, because he was afraid of so much. Fear rode his shoulders, and she didn't know how he even breathed.

Still looking out at the islands, she replied very quietly, "I met her."

Silence stretched between them like a taut string. If either of them was careless, this conversation would snap back and strike them in the face. Leo would not be the first to respond to such a ridiculous comment. He must fear if he said anything that would betray Cora's presence, then he would fall right into Freya's trap.

He cleared his throat and replied, "Met who?"

"Cora."

The physical reaction to her name was violent. He recoiled from the word as though the sound was a poisonous snake. He feared even hearing the name of the woman he had once loved.

What a horrible way to live.

He struggled for long moments, opening his mouth, then closing it again. His beautiful smooth brow furrowed with the weight of his emotions, and Freya knew this was more difficult for him than any of them had imagined.

Her father was right. The Summer Lord was embarrassed and ashamed to have Cora see him like this. He was supposed to be this powerful being who could take on anyone that threatened the Summer Court. And instead, he had turned to alcohol to ease the stress of his responsibilities.

Finally, Leo found the words he wanted to say, and they weren't at all what Freya had hoped. "There are many Elven women by that name. I'm afraid you'll have to be more specific than that."

"We both know you're being deliberately obtuse. We found a way to the isles, and we survived all those horrible creatures you placed in our way. And then we met Cora. She's a beautiful woman now, and she's been alone for a very long time." Freya squeezed her hands together, so she didn't slap Leo at the thought of how long he'd made Cora linger. "She doesn't want to live there anymore, and she's feeling the same thing you are. The elements are going to take back what they gave you, Leo."

"Then let them," he snarled. "Maybe she deserves the title. I could see her ruling this land well, but not me. I wasn't cut from the same cloth as the other Summer Lords. Never have been. And as such, I have been nothing more than a disappointment to this title. They will wipe my name from the history books when this is over."

"When it's over?" she repeated, her voice a hushed whisper. "You are giving up your own life and the woman you love, simply because you are not willing to rise to the occasion?"

He looked at her, then. His feet whipped through the sand that sprayed up behind him in a beautiful golden arc of color. The sun struck his handsome face, his dark features like something out of a storybook. The Summer Lord was one of the most handsome men she had ever met, and that included Eldridge. So why wouldn't Leo just accept that he had a place in this world?

This injury to his soul was deeper than she thought. Freya would need to find out where it had stemmed from. Why he drank. So many questions that needed answering, but this was her moment alone with him.

He stared down at her with spite in his eyes, jaw set, and hands fisted. "I cannot rise to this challenge. It's not as simple as you think."

"Because you are afraid." Freya nodded. "I know what that fear feels like."

They weren't the words he'd expected from her, clearly. Leo opened his mouth, ready to argue with her, but then all the wind in his sails died. "What did you say?" he asked.

"I'm the Queen Killer," she replied with a chuckle. "I defeated the Goblin King, then the Queen. And then I went to the Spring Maiden's court, and I caught her in an elaborate lie to prevent my family from ever finding each other. The expectations of what I will do next are infinite."

"I don't understand why that would make you feel fear." He glared as only the fae could. Leo obviously believed his issues were far more difficult than hers, and maybe they were.

But that didn't mean she couldn't sympathize with him.

"All of these titles are adding up. I have become something of legend to some people I meet, and all the court leaders are afraid of me. Because I did run through your courts and dismantle everything that you knew and loved." Freya opened her hands wide, palms facing him. "But I am a mortal woman. I grew up as a peasant on the edge of the forest, worrying about what I would eat the next day. I don't know how to be this terrifying creature all of you seem to think I am. Luck is on my side. Most of the time. That's the only way I've gotten to where I am."

Leo's eyes widened, then turned into a deep golden hue. "You fear everyone will soon think you are a fraud."

She nodded. "And now you know my secret, Summer Lord. I understand that you are afraid of what she will think when she sees you again. And that someday, she might wake up and realize that you are nothing more than what she feared you were. The terror of your loved one suddenly becoming a stranger is a horrible one to face."

And there was the real secret. Someday, perhaps in a few months or in a few years, Eldridge would roll over and see that she wasn't what he thought she was. That she was an unimpressive woman who had stumbled into the faerie realms, and who had no right to remain.

The Goblin King had helped her every step of the way, and without him, she would still be under the Spring Maiden's spell. And no one would ever have found her.

"Then you do understand." His gaze saw too much. The Summer Lord looked right through her and into her very soul.

He saw that she feared losing the man she loved, and that she wasn't good enough for the person who loved her. He must have known that from the very first moment he saw her. She wasn't a faerie. She wasn't anyone other than Freya, and someday that might not be enough to keep Eldridge at her side.

Leo reached for her hand and grasped it in his own. "We have had our differences, Queen Killer, Defeater of the Goblin King, and Spring Maiden Truth Sayer. But hear me when I say this now. I will put aside what happened in the past because we are so similar in the present."

Goodness, he was a compelling man when he wasn't soaked in alcohol.

To her great embarrassment, tears built in her eyes. Freya realized that this was the first time any faerie had ever forgiven her for what she'd done. And she was intensely aware that her first trip through the faerie courts had been anything but polite or helpful. She had wreaked havoc throughout all the courts. To hear that he forgave her for that, for stealing from him, lying to him, manipulating his court...

It healed a hole in her heart.

She squeezed his hand in her grip. "Good. I'm afraid I needed to hear that more than I want to admit."

"That is quite all right," he replied, releasing her instantly. "Now, if you don't mind my absence, there are a few bottles of wine in my room that are waiting for me."

He turned to leave and Freya's jaw dropped.

That was it? He was going to walk away from her and get drunk after all that had been said?

"Where are you going?" she asked, clarifying, because he couldn't have said what she heard.

"To get very, very drunk, Freya." The Summer Lord's shoulders rounded in on himself, as though he knew what he said was wrong. That the alcohol wouldn't help his situation and only bury these emotions under deep layers of wine and mead.

"No, you aren't." She planted her fists on her hips and drew on every motherly instinct inside herself. "You're going to stay here and talk with me. You need to go see Cora. She's been waiting for you for two hundred years, Leo. You owe her at least a single meeting."

He shook his head. "No. No, I will not be doing that. She will stay on that isle, far from where I can harm any remaining memories of what we once were. What we could have been."

"You deny yourself happiness, and for what?" She threw her hands up in the air. "Because you don't fully believe that you're worthy?"

"Yes!" He spun around again, shouting the word so that it echoed over the waves. "I am undeserving! For what I have done to this court, to her, to myself! She would be better off dead then shackled to me for all eternity."

Freya refused to believe him. Not when she had gotten a glimpse of the man he could be, the one who had so much potential. "At least send her handmaidens, damn it! She's been living out there on her own for far too long!"

Though his eyes widened at the thought, he at least nodded. "Sure. If that's what she wants, then she can have that. But she cannot have me."

The Summer Lord walked away. And though she should have been disappointed, Freya felt as though she had won.

CHAPTER 18

Freya made her way back to their room, hoping that Eldridge would be there so she could share everything that happened. Of course, not the conversation with her father. Eldridge still didn't know she'd found her dad, and that made things even more difficult.

Leo was ashamed to see Cora, and that was an emotion both she and Eldridge could work on. Leo was a decent man. He had grown up in strange circumstances, certainly, but that didn't mean he was any less worthy of a wife.

At least he'd agreed to send Cora handmaidens. And the more Freya thought about it, the more that sounded like the best plan. Two hundred years alone on an island was bound to make a person a little unusual. It would be easier for Cora to dip her toes back into being around this many people. A few hand-maidens would ease her into being around others before she dove headfirst back into the life of the court.

Pushing open the door to their room, Freya thumbed her bottom lip in thought. "Eldridge?" she called out. "I have developments I think you need to hear."

He was sitting on the corner of the bed, hunched over something he held in his hands. It looked like a child's keepsake, some-thing he might have found in the library. And if that tiny box held the key to everything, perhaps the reason why Leo had decided to drink his feelings away, then that was the greatest find they'd have.

"What did you get?" she asked, taking a few rapid steps forward.

Eldridge flinched in on himself and pocketed the item. "Nothing."

"What do you mean, nothing? I just saw you holding it." She held out her hand, fully expecting him to set whatever magical item he'd found in her palm. "Let me see! Did you find some-thing in the library that might help us?"

"No. I found something that means a lot to me, and me alone." He furrowed his brows in a glare. "And perhaps to Cora, if I think about it hard enough. She'll need to see it before you do."

Why wasn't he including her in this? Freya thought they had already worked through him, telling her all the things that she needed to know so they could continue working together, and not apart.

Her heart stuttered in her chest. This was an item that meant a lot to both Eldridge and Cora. So it was something from their childhood, but something that Eldridge didn't want Freya to see. He wanted to share that first with the young woman on the island.

It shouldn't have stung so much. Freya knew that a childhood friend might reminisce easier than her. And that wasn't all so surprising. If she'd found a toy that she and the local boys in her village used to play with, she wouldn't want to talk to Eldridge about it. Such a conversation would feel foolish.

But she still very much wanted to know what it was. She wanted to share her life with Eldridge and every bit of what he'd experienced.

Apparently, he didn't feel the same.

Licking her lips, she tried to distract herself by telling him what had happened. "I, um... I spoke with Leo."

"You what?" His shuttered expression narrowed in on her, the sharp focus sending her back a few steps. "What did he say? What did you say?"

Well, now she couldn't tell him what she'd said. She didn't want to share those personal feelings in her chest when he was already hiding what was in his pocket from her. Though, apparently, Cora was good enough to know what the item was.

Bristling, Freya ground her teeth together before responding. "It doesn't matter. The conversation didn't go as planned. He's still refusing to see her, but he has agreed to send handmaidens to the island. In the long and short of things, I figured that was best. Then Cora can get used to being around so many people again."

"That's genius." He reached for her and swung her into his arms. Eldridge lifted her into the air by the waist, then tucked her against his heart with a spin. "You are a genius. Yes, that's what we need. Leo needs to send some people for her to get comfortable, and then with his court returning and speaking of how kind she is, he'll eventually be tempted enough to return to the isle."

How kind Cora was?

Yes, Freya knew that was the truth. Of course it was. She needed to step away from all this so she didn't turn into a green goblin from the jealousy, however.

She knew he didn't mean to make her jealous. Cora was a dear friend, and that was all. But she still was aching to know what he hid in his pocket, why Cora needed to see it, and why Freya couldn't.

Freya pulled herself out of his arms and smiled at him, although the expression felt as fragile as a spiderweb. "I didn't get through the entire faerie realm without learning to keep a few tricks up my sleeve."

"And don't I know it. You magical woman." He pressed a

hand to his chest. "I'll go with the handmaidens and Arrow to help prepare Cora for what she should expect. You know the dog is so good at wooing the women. And since you've already worn down Leo's defenses, you can stay here and keep working on convincing him to see Cora. Everything is falling into place."

Was it?

Freya wanted to argue with him, but Eldridge was already leaving. He strode out of the door while waving his hand over his head.

He called out one final time, "I'll take care of gathering the handmaidens! We'll return in a fortnight, my love. Don't you worry about a thing!"

And then he was gone.

Two weeks.

Two weeks without him, all because she'd told him what had happened between her and Leo.

"Wait, Eldridge, I thought..." He was already out of the room by the time she found her voice. The words fell flat with no one to hear them, and anxiety melted over her entire body in a wave of sudden discomfort.

All she wanted was to feel a little more confident to let him go. And she realized that was a lot to ask. He was a busy man and wanted to get this over with so they could return to his court. Really, she should be thankful that he was here at all. Everyone needed help from the Goblin King. Or at least, she supposed they would. He'd never told her about what he did as the king.

She stared around the empty room and a horrible sense of foreboding shadowed her mind. She was going to be the only person in this room for two weeks. Two weeks of rolling over and reaching for him in bed, finding only the cold, empty space where he once had been. Two weeks of wondering where he was, if he was missing her too, and if maybe he wasn't.

Heavens above, she was going to lose her mind without him.

And that was even more terrifying than knowing he wouldn't be with her. Since when was she afraid to be alone?

She couldn't stay in this room and wonder what was going to happen next. She just couldn't. Freya had to get up and do something, or she would sit here in the shadows and berate herself until the sun set.

So she fled. Her feet took her through the hallways of the palace in a near run. Flower petals fell on top of her head as if the very soul of this castle was trying to make her feel better. All the hydrangeas that grew up the walls glowed brighter blue in the hopes that their pretty colors would make her smile. Instead, all she could feel was a sense of numbing pain that drowned out everything.

She burst out of the castle to a large room that opened up in the center. It was the floating staircase that led to a crumbling part of the castle. The same place where she had first felt something other than hatred for the Goblin King. He'd dressed her up there in a gown the color of the ocean, and he'd made her feel like someone important in his life.

Of course her feet had brought her here. This was where she had felt the closest to the man she loved.

Sighing, Freya strode around the crumbling structure and realized there was already someone here. A dark skinned someone who was tucked into the moss at the base of a half wall with three bottles of wine situated next to him.

The last person she wanted to see was Leo. He was the reason she was here, and they were all in some sense of turmoil. The ridiculous Summer Lord couldn't pull himself together, and that somehow had translated into her own relationship falling apart.

But those bottles of wine could tempt her. Even a single sip from one of those might make her feel a little better.

"Leo," she said with a grumble.

"I don't care to see you again so soon after our last conversation." He gestured at her with the bottle of wine, swinging it around himself. "You are not my favorite person. If you're having trouble, you can find somewhere else to mope."

"I don't care that you feel that way." She crossed her arms over her chest and tried to look anywhere but at him. Unfortunately, that wouldn't get her anywhere considering they were in a small mossy garden and the only thing in this room was the structure he leaned against. "Besides, I'm trying to hide too."

"Then get your own castle." The sound of a deep swig of wine followed his words, then the faintest smack of lips. "I'm trying to drink in peace."

"Why? Will your own court not even drink with you anymore?" She wouldn't be surprised. The elves could only condone his behavior for so long before they too would grow weary.

"Something like that." There was a tone in his voice that made her turn around. A sadness that leached through every word and a self hatred that made her concerned.

Freya looked him over and realized the Summer Lord looked worse than usual. His clothing was rumpled, his pants creased beyond fixing and his shirt hanging ripped over one shoulder. His eyes were bleary, as if he'd already been drinking for far too long.

She heaved a great sigh and walked over to his side. "You know, it doesn't matter if you want me here or not. I am, and I suppose you'll just have to deal with that."

"I wanted to be alone." He touched the mouth of the bottle to his lips, but this time he didn't drink. "Privacy is impossible to find in this castle, though."

"Privacy? As the Summer Lord? That sounds like a novel idea, but a fantasy nonetheless." Freya wiggled her fingers in front of him, gesturing for him to hand her a bottle. "Give me one."

"They're all mine."

"And yet, you are going to hand me one because I have also had a very difficult day." And if he didn't hand her one, she planned on lunging for a bottle and then he'd have to fight her. Considering the state he was in, she thought she had a good chance of beating him.

Leo eyed her and seemed to understand that was the case. He sighed and handed her a bottle. "What happened to you, then?"

"Do you care to hear?" She took a deep drink of the wine and tried very hard not to cough. What was this oil slick fluid? It was disgusting but burned quite satisfyingly on the way down.

"I find that I'm interested." At the sound of surprise that crossed her lips, Leo looked over at her and shrugged. "I don't have to wallow in my self pity all the time, you know. Maybe I'll feel better if I hear someone else struggling as horribly as I am."

"Struggling?" She wanted to argue that she most certainly wasn't, but look at where she was.

Freya had wandered through the castle to this forgotten place because she wanted to cry over the memory of what she and Eldridge had once had. Like a sad sap of a person. She took another deep swallow and then nodded.

"I suppose I am," she muttered.

And that was the worst thing about all of this. She should be able to be fine without him. Eldridge hadn't come into her life until she was much older, and yes, that was probably a bad thing. She should have gotten married to some lonely farmer who wouldn't have given her any adventure, but he at least would have left her alone to do whatever she wanted.

Instead, she had to find herself in the faerie realm where she shouldn't be. No husband. No family that still relied on her. Instead, she was going to wander through this magical world until she died.

"I'm going to be alone forever," she muttered into the bottle. "Eldridge is leaving with the handmaidens to go back to the isle with Cora. He had something in his hand when I walked into our room. No idea what it was, but he said Cora had to see it."

"She has that way about her, always has. Even when she was a child, she would end up convincing everyone around us to love her more than anyone else in the room." He shook his head, eyes still unfocused with the memory. "It was why I fell in love with her back then, you know. She captured my attention just as she did everyone else."

"I worry that he's going to be on that island without me and forget. That's what he said we needed to do with you. Get you to Cora so you would be in her presence and all those emotions would come back." She swallowed the bitter taste of her fear. "What if two weeks away from me makes him forget how he feels?"

"I never forgot. Not even for a second. I dreamt about her for the first hundred years, and even now I feel like I see her out of the corner of my eye sometimes. You don't forget someone you truly love." Leo tightened his hand so much around the neck of the bottle that the glass shattered with a stunning crack.

They both stared at the mess and the blood leaking between his fingers in silence. Freya knew she should jump to help him and insist that he get the cut cleaned. But she stayed frozen, instead.

"We're both a sad pair," she muttered. "No one should be able to make us feel like this. Not without our permission, at least."

"That's what love does." Leo dropped the shards in disgust. "It twists your damn mind and convinces you that life isn't worth living without them. When in reality, we're better off on our own."

No, she couldn't believe that. No matter how badly this stung, she also realized what a blessing it was to have Eldridge in her life.

Reaching forward, she grabbed his hand and dabbed at it with the tails of her shirt. "You don't actually believe that."

He looked up at her and the sadness in his gaze made her heart ache. "No, I don't. I still love her more than life, but that terrifies me."

She sighed. "Me too. Love is terrifying and wonderful and horrible all at the same time."

Without hesitation, Leo reached for another bottle and clinked it with hers. "Then I suppose all we can do now is drink."

"I suppose you're right." But it sure would make for a very long night.

CHAPTER 19

"My answer is still no," Leo snarled.

And that wasn't a satisfactory answer, nor the one Freya wanted to hear. She pulled harder on his arm and continued dragging him through the halls to her private rooms.

It had been one week since Eldridge left with the handmaidens. An entire week of horrible conversations with Leo that ripped at every insecurity the both of them had. She didn't know if they were healing with each other, or just digging knives into each other's wounds. But whatever they were doing had worked on bringing the two of them a little closer together.

Close enough that she felt comfortable dragging him through the hall like an infant while she argued that it had been far too long since he'd talked with the trees. That was all they wanted from him. A conversation. A chance for him to listen to what they had to say without alcohol running through his veins and making him an insufferable ass.

Yes, she had called the Summer Lord an ass to his face. And she was proud of it.

Leo grabbed onto the doorframe and dug his heels into the floor. "Absolutely not! Freya, would you listen to me? The moment I step foot into that forest, the trees will string me up with their roots and add me to their collection of dead things."

"How do you know that?" She tugged harder on his arm. "I think they want to talk with you, otherwise they would have killed you a long time ago!"

"They have been biding their time for the right moment. And apparently the right instrument of destruction came in the package of a mortal woman." He tugged back, dragging her across the floor toward him. "You're going to get me killed."

Perhaps there was the slightest chance of that happening, but Freya was pretty sure she had a good handle on what the forest wanted. It didn't want to kill Leo, otherwise it never would have sent her on this wild goose chase to convince him to be a better man. If the forest had wanted him dead, then he would be dead.

To her, it sounded like the forest was a lot more interested in getting to know Leo. It wanted him to find out who he was, and to rejoice in the man he could be. Sure, it would be a lot of work to pull himself out of this hole that he'd dug. But that didn't mean it was impossible to do.

She tugged again, much harder this time while throwing her entire body weight into the movement. "I'm right. You're wrong. You're coming with me no matter what."

The veins in his arms stood out as he forcibly held himself in place. "That's hilarious, but no. I'm not. You are but one tiny woman and I am the great Summer Lord. You will not force me to go anywhere with you."

Like the forest had been waiting for his words, the floor opened up beneath them and swallowed both of them. Freya tumbled through the dark, clutching his arm with an iron grip. She wouldn't lose him even when her stomach had shoved its way into her throat. She would hold on until they both struck the ground.

And they hit hard.

All the breath whooshed out of her lungs in one great heave as they struck the earthen floor near the great tree. Wheezing, she pressed her hands to her chest and forced her lungs to inhale. She had to breathe. Why couldn't she breathe?

Leo was making similar horrible sounds, but he at least reached over and slapped her back three times. At the impact, her lungs heaved in the air finally.

She staggered to her feet and held her hand out for him to take. Leo glared at her, choosing to remain on the ground.

"See?" he gasped. "The forest wants me dead."

A stirring at the base of the tree revealed the moss covered body that the tree used to speak. The man's angry expression was only the beginning of a scolding Freya was certain would make her cheeks burn. "If I wanted you dead, then you would be. You stupid little boy. But you deserved to be rattled around before you talked with me again."

Leo's cheeks darkened with what Freya could only hope was embarrassment.

Before he could say something insulting and get himself killed, Freya stepped in front of him and bowed to the dead man. "As always, it's a pleasure to see you."

"The taste of your lies is very sweet, Freya, but we both know it's no sweeter to me than a rotting pumpkin." The man still grinned, however. "Thank you for bringing my boy to see me, though. It's been a very long time since Leo and I have had a conversation."

"For good reason!" Leo staggered to his feet and wiped a hand across his mouth. "You'd rather have me dead than on that throne."

"You know that's not true. But it's easier to say that than to admit you've disappointed me." The man struggled in the roots of the tree, then yanked a skeletal arm from the thick moss. He pulled away from the bark and the rubble until he ripped himself to standing.

Freya tried very hard not to shudder at the sight of a corpse walking toward Leo with single minded intent. The man's bright green eyes glowed as he reached his fingers for the Summer Lord.

"Wait," she croaked. "You aren't going to kill him, are you?"

The corpse turned its head and stared at her with an unimpressed look. "After all the talking we've done, Miss Freya, do you believe I want him dead?"

No. She didn't. Otherwise, she never would have brought the Summer Lord here. This tree wanted to talk with someone it loved very dearly.

She gulped, then replied, "No. I don't think you want to hurt him."

"Then go talk with your own father. He's been waiting for a while to speak with you."

To speak with her? All the blood drained from her face at the mere thought. He was ready to talk? Had the tree healed him so thoroughly?

Summer Lord forgotten, she turned away from the corpse and the faerie. Instead, her eyes found the prison and the dark form hidden in the shadows. She walked toward the small room as though she were in a dream.

What would she even say to her father? That she'd missed him? That seemed too easy. Of course she had missed him. How many years had it been since she'd seen him or her mother? Ten? Eleven? Freya couldn't even think through the passage of time and the worst of it all was her fear that he didn't remember any of the time being gone?

Tears gathered in her eyes. She wrapped her hands around the roots of the prison and watched as a man stood up in the back corner. He turned around and all parts of the wolf were gone. It was her dad staring back at her with a hesitant smile on his face.

He didn't know what to say either, it seemed. For a while they just stared at each other.

Finally Freya croaked, "Can I come in?"

"I think the tree will let you."

The roots shifted, and she flew across the small room. Freya threw her arms around his neck and buried her face in his chest. He still smelled like her father, with the sweet scent of hay and fresh grass. His arms were strong as they wrapped around her, clutching his daughter to his chest.

The sound of his heartbeat was all she'd ever wanted to hear again. This was her father, finally, alive and well when she had been so certain he was dead.

"Dad," she whispered again. "I didn't think I'd ever see you again."

"I was certain you were right only a few days ago." He pressed his lips to the top of her head, tightening his grip on her. "Oh my sweet, brave Freya. You've grown so much."

Goodness, she must have. The last time he saw her, she was nothing more than a teenager. The same age as Esther, who still had more growing to do. Freya pulled away so she could look at him, reaching to pat her hands on his cheeks. "And you got older."

The silver streaks at his temples looked handsome, though. She thought her mother would very much like the change when she saw him again.

Her father tilted his head back and let out a clap of booming laughter. She'd forgotten how loud the sound was. How he could fill a room with happiness with the sound of his laugh. "Oh, I'm sure I look older. You don't have to point it out though, darling."

She laughed with him and it felt like the most natural thing in the world. They spoke as if no time had passed between the time they had last seen each other, and it felt like she had seen him yesterday. All the anger she might have directed at him melted away, knowing that he was alive. That he wasn't the werewolf any longer.

The werewolf. A shiver ran through her with the knowledge that it might not actually be gone. She had to ask. She had to know.

"Is the wolf..." Freya cleared her throat and took a step back.

"Is the tree holding the wolf at bay? Or do you have it under control?"

The frown on his face suggested she wouldn't like the answer he was about to give her. "Both," he replied. "The tree is helping me keep control, but I am learning how to hold it back. The wolf is difficult to understand. And I grew up with people like this. Wolves who lived in hiding and no one would ever have guessed they were afflicted by this curse but... I didn't realize how hard it was for them."

She could only imagine it would feel like denying himself food or water. The wolf was a part of him, not just another being.

He shook his head and held out his hand for her to take. "Come here, darling. Tell me what I've missed and then we'll talk about the wolf. I'm not leaving here for a little while longer, and I need to know how you found me and if... if..."

He couldn't say her mother's name. She knew that would be difficult for him, but she hadn't guessed how choked up it would make him.

Freya took her father's hand and let him guide her to the back of the prison where he'd set up a small table and some chairs. A cot rested in the corner, all human furniture now that he wouldn't destroy them in the form of a wolf. "Mother?"

Her father sat down and briefly nodded. Although, he couldn't look her in the eye now that he thought of the woman he loved.

"She's alive." Freya joined him at the table. "I found her first. You led me to her."

"I did?" He breathed a long sigh of relief. "I thought I remembered seeing her while I was the wolf, but sometimes that's not a good sign. I had hoped... Well. I had hoped that she was still alive and that the wolf hadn't done something we both would regret."

"No. You saved her. You saved all of us."

Freya let the story pour out of her lips like a dam had broken open. She told him everything she and Esther had done when they realized their parents were gone. She told him about Esther and that stupid necklace, and how she'd beaten the Goblin King. She told him about saving the faerie courts and bringing back their rightful ruler, only to realize that her mother was under the Spring Maiden's thumb.

Not a single detail was spared, and she probably told him too much information by the end. She feared his head would spin with all the stories she'd told him, but instead, her father stared at her with wide, proud eyes.

"You did all that in my absence?" he asked.

"I did." She tucked a strand of hair behind her ear and tried not to let exhaustion overwhelm her. "It wasn't easy. I'm sorry if I told the story wrong and made you think that I could do it all on my own. I had a lot of help along the way."

"Yes, you did. I think I'd like to meet this goblin dog. He seems like my kind of person." Her father tapped a finger to his chin. "Although this Goblin King... I'll wait to decide if I like him."

She wouldn't expect any different. Freya chuckled. "He's a good man. I don't know where I stand with him right now. That's not his fault, that's my own."

"Is it?" Her father reached across the table and caught her hands in his. "I know you will do this, and you will succeed. Because you're my daughter. There is nothing in this realm that could stop you."

His words lifted her up and gave her a confidence she'd been missing. Freya straightened her shoulders and felt power return to her veins. "I can. And I will."

"Good girl." Her father released her hands and nodded back toward the Summer Lord. "You might want to gather him up now, child. He looks well and thoroughly scolded."

She looked over her shoulder and thought Leo looked a little green. He might have looked drunk if she didn't know he was stone cold sober.

Sighing, she stood up and dusted her hands off on her hips. "You're right. I need to take him home. But..."

What words could ever explain how she felt? How her heart was healed at the sight of him?

He smiled at her. "I'll see you again, Daughter. I have no doubt in that."

Freya pressed a hand to her thundering heart. "I'll see you soon, Dad. I swear it."

CHAPTER 20

Freya teleported to her room in the Summer Palace and landed on her back hard with the Summer Lord at her side. She wore a dazed expression that she wasn't proud of. But what was a girl supposed to do?

Her father was not only well and alive, he was talking to her like a normal father would. He had laughed with her, joked, and listened to her stories. Freya was elated that he was back to himself. Except now there was a whole new host of issues that she had to overcome. What would her mother think when she saw her father again? Would Esther even remember him?

Why wasn't she angry at her father the same way she had been angry at her mother?

Huffing out a breath, she looked over at Leo to see how he was handling things. Considering his face was ashen and his brows furrowed, he appeared to be handling his own situation even worse. Good, at least he was in the same place she was in mentally.

Freya reached out and patted his shoulder. "How are you holding up?"

"Not well."

"That tree really gave it to you, huh?"

She waited for the words to sink in before tilting her head back and laughing. They both chuckled through the pain until they settled back onto the floor in twin heaps.

"Yes," Leo replied. "The tree really gave it to me. I haven't been scolded like that since I was a child, and the last person to do it was..."

At his hesitation, Freya filled in the blank for him. "The tree?"

"The tree. I suppose there's only been one person daring enough to scold me like I was a petulant child." He touched a hand to his chest, right over his heart. "I suppose I still am that angry little boy who wanted to yell at his parents for not giving him all the things he wanted. That's rather frustrating, you know."

"No personal growth is simple." She pillowed her head on her arm, rolling so she could stare at him. "I know it's not easy, but change isn't something to fear. You could be someone great. Someone better."

"What if I don't like that new version of myself?" His troubled expression deepened. "What if that person is someone I don't recognize?"

"I think if you met yourself when you were a child, you'd be annoyed to see that you were a very different person then as well. We all change and grow. That's how life works." Even she had changed, drastically.

Sometimes it still startled Freya to think about how much she had changed. But then again, that was the same situation Leo was having. He didn't want to believe he wasn't the same person he used to be.

He hummed deep in this throat before nodding. "It's something I'll consider, mortal. Thank you."

Well, she hadn't expected his thanks. But she'd take it.

Freya pushed up onto her hands and knees. "That's that, then. I suppose we have to find something else to do to bide our time. I'm ready to have Eldridge back, and I'm sure you're dreading the stories from the isle."

"The tree wanted me to tell you something, too." Leo put his hand on her arm, forcing her to stop and look at him. "There is a method of finding out the secrets of others. It's... Well the fae don't use it. It's backfired one too many times for us. But the tree said you might need it."

"Excuse me?" She didn't want to admit that made her frightened. All the blood drained from her face and she felt light headed.

Why did the tree think she needed to reveal someone's secrets? Why would it even want her to have that ability?

"Water in the Summer Court holds an immense amount of power. And since your father was a changeling here, and absorbed some of that magic to pass down to you, there is a chance you could use the pools to see what you want." Leo released her, and his expression said he was uncomfortable even telling her this. "It said you have already seen how some might use their magic in the pools to communicate, or perhaps see the future. But the tide pools can also be used to spy."

The temptation was so great it made her fingers curl into her palms. No, she wouldn't entertain this thought at all. Eldridge wasn't doing anything that he shouldn't and even assuming he might be was the greatest betrayal of their relationship thus far.

She clenched her jaw so hard it made her teeth hurt. "I don't foresee myself needing to use that."

"Regardless, if you wanted to spy, all you would have to do is find a glassy surface of water and ask to see what you wanted to see." He rolled onto his feet and then held out his hand for her to take. "Come on. Considering the warning, I thought you might like to go to the isle now."

"I don't want to go across those waters alone." She took his hand and let him drag her to her feet. "I will wait for Eldridge to come back."

"Then don't." He sheepishly ran a hand over his head before

gesturing for her to follow him. "I should have told you a long time ago, but there's another way to get to the isles. It's just... not well known. I'm the only one who's supposed to use it."

Curiosity would always be her downfall. Freya followed him all the way through the halls, touching her fingers to the glowing plants that lit up the hallways. They reached for her now with friendly whispers, unlike the first time she'd been here when she was certain the plants would kill her if she touched them.

They were kinder. Softer. More likely to give her a little room to breathe if she needed it. Although, she hated to think that was all changing simply because she'd created a tentative friendship with the Summer Lord. She still planned on making him marry Cora. For the good of the court.

Leo stopped in front of a door hidden in the wall. Ivy covered it so thickly that she would have walked past it if she hadn't been told it was there. He reached into his pocket and drew out a small skeleton key. "This will only open the door once every five days."

Surprising. If this room held a portal, then why wouldn't it open as many times as he wanted?

Freya stayed quiet as he swung the door open and revealed a hidden pool of water. Light glowed from deep underneath the still surface, spilling out over the mossy floor and up into the tendrils of ivy hanging from the ceiling.

"What is this place?" she asked.

"A portal room." Leo tucked his hands behind his back and strode toward the water with a slight saunter to his step. "I'm certain you've never seen such a thing before, and that's unsurprising. After all, the Summer Court is so much more beautiful than the other courts. We know what it means to have some sense of aesthetic."

She didn't agree with him, but she couldn't argue over the beauty of this place. All the other portals she had seen were built out of wind and magic. But this one? This was the very ocean waiting to be used at the whim of the Lord.

She stepped close to the edge and peered into the water. "Where does it go?"

"There's another one on the isle, within the cliff side village that I'm sure you visited." He joined her hesitantly, almost like he was afraid of what he would see staring back at him. "All you have to do is step into the water and then you'll be there. It's that easy."

Sure. Easy to him. But Freya feared what would happen if she walked into the water and the magic realized that she wasn't the Summer Lord, or even fae.

Gulping, she stepped onto the edge and held out her arms for balance. "It's not going to spit me back out because I'm not you, right?"

"There's only one way to find out. Oh, and tell Cora I'm coming to visit her soon. It's long pastime we met again." Leo's wicked grin only served to make her even more nervous. He stepped up to her side, planted his hand on her back, and shoved.

Freya fell into the water with a horrible belly flop that stung her skin even through the thin skirts she wore. The water rushed up her nose and pressed into her lungs. She floundered for a second underneath the water, not knowing which way was up. Blinking through the saltwater, she searched for the light of the portal room.

Her gut said this was no portal. Leo had played a grand jest, but she didn't want to drown before she made it to the isles. Swimming to the surface, she spluttered as cool air blasted her face.

"Damn it, Leo!" she snarled, blinking through the painful drops of saltwater. "I didn't want to get wet!"

But Leo never responded.

Freya swam to the edge of the pool and hauled herself onto the lip. Sitting, she scrubbed her eyes to clear her vision and was shocked to see white-washed walls and sunlight glittered through the tiny chips of seashells embedded in the stone.

She was on the island. And without having to go past those terrifying crabs and sharks again.

This would have been so much easier to get to their destination the first time. Poor Arrow. There was no need for him to be as sick as he had gotten, and the days of complaining she'd endured afterward.

Freya swung her legs over onto the floor at the same time the doors slammed open and Cora came rushing in. Half her hair was braided, the other side a plume of dark curls that coiled around her skull. "Leo? Leo, is it really you?"

The other woman's expression fell when she caught sight of Freya.

"Sorry to disappoint." Freya lifted a wet arm and waved. "He sent me."

Cora sighed and crossed her arms over her chest. "Why am I not surprised? Of course he sent you. He'll do anything to avoid seeing me again, won't he?"

Freya stood and wrung the water out of her skirts. She'd need something else to wear, and fast. Her teeth chattered already. "He said to let you know that he is coming soon. He wants to see you, Cora. He's just scared."

"Of what?" Cora threw her arms into the air. "Never mind, I don't want to know. So much has happened since you were here last, and I think you should see it all. Your Goblin King is a resourceful man, and the handmaidens are hard workers. We're all ready to welcome the Summer Lord should he ever decide he wants to see me. Or even step up to the throne the trees gifted him."

Apparently Cora had been talking with Eldridge too much. The sting of her words would be heartbreaking if Leo heard them. The poor man needed someone who would see him and forgive all the actions he'd taken. Or at least set them aside until he grew more confident. His misguided choices were the very reason he had avoided seeing her for such a long time.

"He's trying his best, Cora. You need to be gentle with him

when he does come to see you." She padded over to the elf, wet footsteps slapping the stone. "The last thing he needs is to think his wife is a harpy."

"A harpy? No, of course not." Cora sniffed and ran a hand over the side of her head that was braided. "He'll be married to an Elven princess, and he better remember that."

Oh no. She had been talking to Eldridge far too much. Freya trailed after the elf, who had suddenly found her aggressive side and wondered how she was going to fix this.

Yes, it was very important that Cora be confident and able to call Leo out when he was doing something that she didn't like. She absolutely should, as well. A partnership was just as much about helping the other person become a better version of themselves as it was supporting each other. However. There was a correct way to do that, with gentleness and understanding. It seemed like Eldridge had convinced Cora to beat Leo over the head with a stick until the Summer Lord broke under the weight of her disappointment.

And that simply wouldn't do.

"Cora," Freya called out. "I think we should talk about Leo before he gets here. There are some things you should know, and understand..."

"I think I understand him perfectly after talking with Eldridge."

Freya muttered under her breath, "You don't. I'm trying to help you, woman."

But of course, she couldn't say that too loud. Not when Cora was clearly happy with this new, confident version of herself. Softening this woman would take time and energy that Freya didn't have right now.

All she wanted was to see Eldridge. That was it.

"Cora, where is Eldridge?" she called out.

The faint discomfort she'd felt when the trees told her to scry came back. What if Cora acted strangely? What if...

The elf flippantly waved over her shoulder. "Oh, he's around here somewhere. Probably with the handmaidens knowing him. He hasn't left their side since they got here. Everything has been about preparations and I have no idea what he's been planning. The man has been running around here like he's decided to quit being the Goblin King and change his profession to head of household."

That... Didn't sound like Eldridge at all.

Frowning, Freya glanced down one of the village hallways and cleared her throat. "Do you need me now, or might I find the Goblin King?"

"Well, you are here for me, aren't you?" Cora looked over her shoulder and must have seen Freya's expression. The odd, new personality fell from her shoulders. Cora's face softened, and she smiled. "Oh, right. Of course you'd want to see him. It's been a while, hasn't it? Time passes differently for me, and I forget that. Please, Freya. Go steal him away from the handmaidens for a little while. Walk the beach and reconnect."

"Thank you," she whispered, then ran through the nearest home to find her Goblin King.

CHAPTER 21

She found Eldridge in the garden of tide pools outside the cliff village. He was surrounded by jewels of the Summer Court, each handmaiden more beautiful than the last. They were almost blinding in their stunning nature, but Freya didn't want to look at them.

She wanted to look at her Goblin King, who stood in the center of all the chaos with his hands clasped behind his back. His eyes were narrowed on their work, his voice sharp and critical. It almost looked like they were gathering things from the pools, but what could he have found?

"Eldridge!" she called out.

His gaze traveled up to the village, and he stared at her for a few moments before a bright smile crossed his lips. "My darling! What are you doing here? How are you here?"

The steps to walk down were slippery with saltwater and a sticky residue she couldn't name. Freya clambered down them, less than gracefully, but she didn't care who saw her stumble. She wanted to throw her arms around the Goblin King and not let go.

Two weeks had been far too long. And she didn't intend to do that again anytime soon.

With one last trip, she tumbled into his arms. It didn't matter that she wasn't very graceful, or even that she must have looked ridiculous. All that mattered was the way his warm, strong arms came around her and held her close to his heart.

He still smelled like sweet apple pie and cinnamon. Even surrounded by the ocean. And the tittering elves that held their hands to their masks didn't bother her, even though she knew they were watching.

Freya tilted her head back and wrapped an arm around his neck. She drew him down for a deep, long kiss that fueled her soul with each lingering press. "I missed you," she whispered. "I missed you so much."

He drew back with a bemused smile, clearly not sure why she was so clingy. "I missed you as well, my love. But what are you doing here? We had a plan."

"We did." Freya looked around and noted how lovely the sun reflected on the metallic shimmer in the handmaidens' gowns. "I already spoke with Leo, he's coming to visit soon."

"Soon or tomorrow?"

"Soon." She glanced up, then frowned at his expression. "What?"

"Leo is a very good manipulator. He twists words with the best of us and I just... I don't think it's likely that he'll be coming as he said." Eldridge released her and stepped back toward the handmaidens. "Perhaps you should return and force him to come here."

"I believe him." And it made her cheeks heat with anger to think he didn't think she was capable of convincing Leo to come here when that was the only job she'd had. "We struck up a strange sort of friendship in your absence, and I know he's going to come to the isles. He wouldn't have said so if he didn't have the plans in his head."

"Freya, I know you made some kind of friendship, and I'm not surprised by that. The fae seem to love you." He rubbed his cheek, clearly uncomfortable. "But I don't think you know him as well as I do."

"A person can change." She didn't understand why he was so determined to not believe her. Or Leo.

It was like Eldridge had some vendetta against the man. He was so certain that Leo was the same boy who had so disappointed him long ago, that Eldridge couldn't see through the visage Leo had built around himself.

The Summer Lord was a decent man with a weak spirit. But that didn't mean he couldn't change or grow with the right help. Like any tree, he needed a place to put his roots, and then he could flourish with the support of family and friends. Without that support, he would continue to topple over and have to start anew.

"I—" Freya started, only to be interrupted by one of the handmaidens.

"My lord! We've finished gathering all the crystals you requested in the water. What would you like us to do with them?"

Eldridge turned toward them with a bright grin on his face. "Excellent! Bring them to the section of the village we've taken over and we'll start enchanting them. Soon, this isle will glow with lights like the stars!"

The women teetered off, all of their arms overladen with bags of tiny crystals. So that's what they had been gathering. Why there were crystals in tidepools, Freya would likely never know.

"I thought maybe we could take the afternoon together?" Freya was very aware of her sodden dress that likely smelled of seawater. She'd need a bath before they did anything, but she could dunk herself in the ocean again. Or maybe they could swim together.

She would love to have an afternoon swimming in the magical waves with the man she loved. Maybe this was the perfect time to tell him that she was madly, deeply in love with him.

But Eldridge wasn't even looking at her. His eyes were on the handmaidens as they raced toward the opening in the cliff. A thousand thoughts danced behind his eyes and Freya already knew his answer long before he opened his mouth.

"If Leo is coming soon, then we have less time than we thought to prepare. This is the first step toward getting your father back, Freya. The first step toward our future. We can't slow down now." He reached for her hands and squeezed her fingers. "I know it's tough, my love. I also want an afternoon with just the two of us, but we have too much to do."

And then he raced off after the other women without even a second glance back at her.

What was she supposed to do? Freya had nothing that was under her control here. She was left standing on the rocky beach, wondering what had happened that made her feel so... alone.

Wrapping her arms around herself, Freya turned down the beach and started walking. She didn't know where she was going or what plan was in her head. All she knew was that she had to keep putting one foot in front of the other. For a little while at least. Otherwise, all those horrible thoughts would spew out of her mouth.

Logically, she knew Eldridge was right. They needed to figure out this riddle in the Summer Court, although Eldridge had no clue that she'd already found her father. The forest had to be appeased or they would never get him back. And the forest wanted Leo and Cora to accept their rightful place in the court.

And if they didn't, then she might as well give up now and head back to the Goblin Court with her proverbial tail tucked between her legs. She didn't have a luxurious one like her sister, but that didn't mean she wouldn't feel it when she returned to her mother and told her that she'd failed. Her father would likely go back to being a mindless beast slathering in that prison for the rest of his life. And she would never let herself live this down.

Which meant she had to follow the plan. She had to focus now, and then she could figure out what she was doing with her relationship later. It wasn't like they didn't have all the time in the world.

Except they didn't.

She touched a finger to the corner of her eyes where she'd noticed a few crow's feet were already showing. She wasn't that old yet, but she could already see the signs of age. Eventually she would be this ridiculous, old woman limping after a handsome Goblin King. Maybe he would still love her when she looked like that, but maybe he wouldn't want to deal with the pain and discomfort that came with old age.

Freya knew she was spiraling. But she couldn't stop.

She paused next to one of the tide pools and stared down into the crystal clear water. The surface was so smooth it was like a mirror, reflecting her own wide-eyed stare back at her. She looked manic. Mad. Crazed knowing that she couldn't stop the aging that would divide her and the man she loved.

No, she couldn't think like this. Freya tapped the surface of the water and watched the ripples spread from the single tap. If only she could make sure that she wasn't crazy. That he loved her still as much as he said he did.

The temptation to scry rose again. The trees wouldn't have told her to use that magic if they hadn't seen that she would need it. What if they were warning her to look, because something important was happening right underneath her nose?

It was a bad idea. The Goblin King might even feel that she was spying on him, and then how would she explain herself?

Freya still let all the thoughts trickle from her mind and whispered, "Can you show me the Goblin King?"

Guilt already gnawed on her conscious, but she was given the opportunity to prove to herself that the whispers in her mind were nothing more than anxiety. This was all in her head, she had nothing to worry about.

The water shimmered with magic. It wasn't her magic. Freya didn't feel that strange pull on her very life force like it had the few times she'd used her power. This was almost like the Summer Court was showing her what she needed to see.

Suddenly, she wasn't looking at the tiny stones at the bottom of the pool or the crab picking through kelp. Now she was looking at Eldridge as he strode into a room where Cora stood in the center. He held out his arms for the beautiful woman and tucked her against his heart, as he did to Freya when she needed someone to lean on. He whispered something to Cora, who laughed with her entire body.

The scene was innocent. She shouldn't read anything into the body language that they exhibited and yet, she did. Cora was too comfortable. Eldridge was too happy. And she was standing alone on a rocky shore covered in seaweed and saltwater.

Swallowing hard, she whispered to herself, "It means nothing. They're friends. You know they're friends."

But it still hurt to see him hugging Cora. Her heart twisted in her chest knowing that even though this was an act of comfort and excitement that the Summer Lord was finally going to be here, it didn't matter.

Jealousy was a wicked poison that spread through her chest like a wildfire through a dry forest. She couldn't think. She couldn't breathe. All she could do was stare down at the water in shock and horror.

She had to stop or she would surely go mad. She'd rush to the room they were in and slap both of them, making a scene out of nothing.

Freya dashed her hand over the water, slapping the surface so it wouldn't show her that horrible image any longer. If only she could get clarification, hear what Eldridge had said...

She stood back up and pressed a hand to her chest. This was the poison the forest was talking about. The Summer Court was sick, and it was affecting her. She'd never been this jealous woman who wanted to follow her significant other around and limit what they could or could not see.

Freya had never once questioned his adoration or his intention with her. Eldridge was a doting, loving partner who had seen that she needed more reassurance than most. He'd given her that and here she was. Spying. All because there was another beautiful woman around him and she couldn't stand it that she wasn't the prettiest girl in the room.

Freya had never been the prettiest girl.

"You have been surrounded by fae this entire time," she reminded herself. "And he still picked you."

The grubby, strange, arrogant mortal woman who had been bound and determined to hate him no matter how hard he tried to convince her otherwise. Their love hadn't bloomed suddenly or without work. They had struggled through the courts together and...

No. She couldn't do this anymore. She needed to clear her head.

Staring up at the cliff's edge, she resolved herself to being better. She would go back into that village and she would help Cora get ready for the moment when Leo arrived. Then the Lord and Lady could reconcile their broken relationship. The forest would be happy and it would release her father.

Then and only then would she focus on fixing her own relationship with the Goblin King.

CHAPTER 22

"W hen do you think he'll get here?" Cora asked.

The pretty elf looked over her shoulder at Freya, who sat on the side of her bed. Cora was delicately twisting the braids on her head into little bubbles that were both gorgeous and strange to Freya.

She'd offered to help prepare Cora for when the Summer Lord would get here, but Cora had laughed and said Freya wouldn't know how to do her hair. Watching now, Freya realized the other woman was very correct. She had no idea what to do with hair that curly.

So she'd sat on the edge of the bed with her hands under her bottom so she didn't touch anything.

What had Cora just asked? Oh right.

"He didn't say, but considering the rushing handmaidens that keep running through the room, I'm going to guess he's informed them that he'll arrive today." She tucked a strand of hair behind her ear. "He said to tell you that he was coming. I think that bodes well."

"I'm not getting my hopes up." Cora wrung her hands, then finished up the last braid. She kept touching the bubbles on her head, then turned toward Freya with a frown on her face. "Do you think he'll like this? Or should I do something else?"

Considering it had taken many hours to do what she'd already done, Freya wasn't sure she'd have the opportunity to do something different.

But she couldn't tell Cora that. The poor woman would fall into a dead faint.

She stood up and approached Cora with a soft smile on her face. Gently, Freya turned the elf to look into the mirror at her own reflection. "You're a beautiful woman and he loves you already. The sight of you is going to take his breath away, even if you were wearing a burlap sack."

Cora stared at herself and touched a finger to her glistening cheek. "Do you really think that?"

How had Freya ever thought this woman would entertain a relationship with Eldridge? Cora continually made it so very clear that she was in love with Leo. That she would wait for ages until he came to his senses and saw the stunning woman who was in front of him. Waiting for ages so that he would love her the way she loved him.

Freya smiled and patted Cora's shoulder. "I do. I think he's going to walk over the beach and fall to his knees in the sand because he's a fool for waiting this long. You're going to make him so happy. And not by listening to whatever Eldridge told you to do. You'll make him happy just by being yourself."

And there it was. Cora's expression crumbled, and she stared down at her fingers in her lap. How dare Eldridge make her feel like she couldn't be herself!

Freya retreated to the bed and sat down with a hard thump. "What did Eldridge say?"

"He said to be harder than I normally would because it's been two hundred years and I have every right to be angry." Cora met her gaze in the mirror, her expression filled with rage. "And I am furious, Freya. It has taken him this long to come here and... well. What is different this time?"

"The world as the two of you know it might end?" A thousand possibilities came to mind on why he was doing all this, but Freya realized that Cora's anger was justified as well. "I think you can be angry at him and kind at the same time. You don't have to attack him the moment he steps on this isle just because he's made mistakes. He knows that. What he's doing right now is holding out an olive branch so you two might talk about everything that's happened and figure out a way to fix it."

"I don't know how to fix it." Cora lifted her hands as if she had hoped she could grasp something in them. "The threads of our lives are intertwined as no other lives are. I feel the forest wanting to throw him into the ground and I know the sea is angry with me. But what if all this time apart has turned us into very different people? What if neither of us want to be with each other?"

"Then you won't." Freya knew that to be the truth, at the very least. No matter how hard she wanted them to be together, the reality was that no one could force them to fall back in love. "A lot has changed, I agree with that. But if you listen to Eldridge's advice, the first thing that Leo will see is an angry woman who cannot forgive him. That's a lasting memory that will take years, or perhaps centuries, to heal."

"You're right." Cora nodded firmly. "You're absolutely right. I should be myself."

"I think once you two get some time alone, you'll be surprised at how much hasn't changed. Sure, there are a lot of experiences that have made the two of you different people. But I know the children you once were are still in there somewhere. You'll know what to do when you see him."

Freya would have said more, but a pounding knock on the door interrupted her. A handmaiden burst in without waiting for them to call for her.

"The Summer Lord approaches!" she said excitedly. "He's here! He's coming on a ship, with countless other elves from the court behind him!"

Right, well, she should have told him to be a little less showy than that. Poor Cora already looked like she was going to faint.

Freya rolled her eyes up to the ceiling and tried very hard to stay calm and collected. Both fae were centuries older than she was, and they needed their hands held for love. Romance should have been easy for them by now, and instead, they only excelled at mincing words and twisting the truth.

"Everything is going to work out," she said again. "Cora. Listen to me, we need to get you dressed and ready to see Leo. Do you think you can do that?"

Cora's face said she couldn't. Her entire being radiated with fear and discomfort. And Freya didn't blame her.

After all, Cora had been on this isle for two hundred years by herself. Now she had a few handmaidens, and that was likely fun at first. Finally, some people for her to talk to. But the reality of having an entire court on her doorstep, with the man she was supposed to marry... That was a different story.

Freya pinched the bridge of her nose. "You stay here. Get ready and when you are finished, talk with Eldridge. Let him know that I went to greet Leo and I'm getting him settled. We will not push you, Cora. You need to do these things on your own, and only when you are ready."

In the meantime, she had to be the one that raced down the beach like a crazy person. What was Leo thinking? He was going to overwhelm Cora and then they all were going to be sent from this shore. She would end up having to start this process all over again and honestly, Freya was about done with these two love-birds who had no idea what they wanted out of life. Or each other.

"Wait!" Cora called out. "Wait, Freya! I'm coming with you."

Cora stood up and Freya turned to see the Summer Lady standing behind her. And that was exactly what Cora was.

With a simple hand flick, magic poured a golden dress over her skin. The sheer fabric was stunning and looked like molten metal had been formed in the shape of her body. The dress hugged her curves, accentuating her hourglass waist. Her hair was done perfectly, not a strand out of place, and her expression was one of serene confidence.

This was exactly what Freya had thought to find at the hand of the Summer Lord. A Lady who commanded attention, and if a person didn't bend their knee to her, she would summon a storm to sweep them away.

Her eyes must have been bugging out of her head, and maybe that was rude, but Freya couldn't stop staring at Cora.

"My goodness," she whispered. "Look at you."

"Does it look silly?" Cora brushed a hand down her stomach. "I always thought this would be what I wore, but I can change it."

"No. Don't you change a single thing. You look like a goddess." Leo was going to trip over his own tongue when he saw what he'd been missing all this time. The fool had taken far too long, but thank goodness their kind was long lived.

At least, Freya assumed they were. Were the fae immortal, or did they have only a certain length to their life?

She'd have to ask Eldridge. The answer seemed rather important, she'd just never wondered what the truth was before.

Cora swept out of the room with Freya on her tail. Almost all the handmaidens were waiting for her, holding glowing crystals in their hands. "My Lady," one said, holding out a crystal for Cora to take. "We've decorated the entire village with these. It will look like the sun itself shines from your home. He will be so pleased when he sees you."

Though Cora took the offered crystal, there was a darker expression on her face. "Good. I want him to think this isle is beautiful."

Freya read between the lines. The Summer Lady worried that her Lord would find her wanting. And that wasn't fair. Not when there was so much good in her.

She reached out and touched a hand to Cora's back. Whispering so the handmaidens didn't over hear, she said, "You're going to make it through tonight. And then, when it's all said and done, I'll think you'll have found this all very easy."

"Thank you, Freya," Cora replied. "I couldn't do this without you."

They walked through the halls until they met Eldridge, who waited for them at the entrance to the village. He wore his customary black velvet suit with the gold foiled edges, bowing low as they approached. "My Lady. You look exquisite, as always."

"And you flatter me, Goblin King." Cora's cheeks darkened. "But thank you. I believe the Summer Lord will be impressed with the show you have provided."

"It has nothing to do with me, and everything to do with you, if he's impressed. His Lady has been waiting for a very long time, and he needs to see what a fool he was to keep you on this isle when he could have had you by his side." Eldridge's gaze met hers, and he grinned. "Like I feel every time this one lingers too far from my gaze. Freya? A moment, if you would."

Though a part of her very much wanted to hear what he had to say, Freya also feared they would get in an argument. And the frustrated part of her also realized that she was still angry at him for leaving her on the rocky shore when he could have been with her. Just as he wanted to be now.

Instead, she shook her head and nodded toward Cora. "They need us to be there when they finally see each other again, Eldridge. Isn't that what you said when we last spoke?"

His brows drew down as he thought through her words. She could only hope that he wouldn't realize her frustration about how he'd treated her. Because then he would drag her to the side and make her talk about how she was feeling.

Freya wasn't ready to talk about that, yet. She was still frustrated. Angry. Upset. And some of those emotions were her own doing because she had scried and seen them doing things that she didn't like. And sure, that wasn't fair of her to put that on him. But it didn't make it any easier.

"Well," he said, clearing his throat. "Then hold on a second and let me make sure you're presentable to the Summer Lord."

She tried to ignore the disappointment in his eyes as he waved a hand. The magic settled over her shoulders in a wave, and the gown that appeared on her body outdid any magic he'd performed thus far. Like him, she was in dark clothing, but he'd covered the fabric with tiny diamonds that sparkled as she moved. The low neckline was tasteful but still showed off an ample amount of her chest.

She lifted a brow and stared at him, wondering why he'd chosen this dress for her. It certainly showed more of Freya's skin than she was comfortable with. And bare arms?

Cora started off ahead of them as Freya took Eldridge's offered arm. He leaned down and whispered in her ear, "I know this is Cora's moment. But I intend on reminding the Summer Lord that while his bride is beautiful, mine is far more powerful."

She blushed, her cheeks heating unbidden at his words. And it was entirely natural for her entire body to flush when he was that close to her. She missed the feeling of his skin against hers and the way he would chuckle in her ear as he moved above her.

But now was not the time for such thoughts, not when she was already too nervous to think straight.

Freya sighed and tugged him toward the walkway that would lead them to the ocean. "Come on, Goblin King. We need to greet the Summer Lord and make sure these two lovebirds don't kill each other when they do meet after all this time."

He wrapped her hand in his, linking their fingers even as she tugged him to move faster. "The lovebirds should be able to handle themselves considering their advanced age. Are you sure we can't have a few moments to ourselves? I need to talk with you Freya."

And she needed to chew his ear off in anger when they were

finally done with this mess. Didn't he see how mad she was at him? Surely he could sense the anger radiating through her entire body.

"Soon," she replied. "You can have your moment soon, Eldridge."

CHAPTER 23

Freya and Eldridge walked down the beach, hand in hand. She watched the small boats approach in the distance. The Summer Lord had hung lanterns from the bow of each boat, and the bright lights lit their way as the sun set on the horizon. The stars twinkled and all the crystals Eldridge had enchanted gave the entire beach a lovely glow that could not be beaten by any fairytale.

Cora waited at the edge of the shore. The waves kissed her toes with every small movement and she held the crystal in her hand like a candle. This was the kind of scene that inspired artists to paint, Freya was certain of it.

The boats hit the sand and Leo remained standing at the bow. He wore billowing white pants and a golden vest, lacking a shirt. Freya knew he'd done that to show off the muscles of his arms and chest.

Someone had painted gold symbols all down his arms in tiny, decorative marks. She leaned over and whispered, "Do the marks have meaning?"

"They're runes." Eldridge squinted, then smiled softly. "They're for good luck. Clever man, I'm certain she'll remember those."

Freya hoped Cora did. The runes were a cry for pity, or perhaps for the chance to make up for what he'd done. With a swift leap, he struck the waves and waded through them to Cora's side.

No one could say Leo didn't have a flourish in his movements. And the tactic was working on Cora. Her eyes were wide and her mouth dropping open as she watched this prince from the storybooks fall onto his knees before her. Exactly as Freya had said he would.

"My Summer Lady," he said, his words quiet though somehow ringing over the sands. "I have made you wait for too long. I beg your forgiveness, and for a single night to convince you that I am still worthy of your grand attention."

"Is that so?" Cora held the crystal higher so the light could bask on Leo's handsome features. "You have a lot of explaining to do, Summer Lord."

"And anything you ask of me, I will tell." He lifted his head and stared up at her with so much love in his eyes all the women in the crowd swooned. "My greatest mistake was in not finding you sooner, Cora. I'm ashamed to admit I've been hiding. Afraid of what you think of me."

"What changed?"

Leo glanced over at Freya and Eldridge, the flick of his gaze telling in the movement. "A very dear friend reminded me that people can be forgiven, and that sometimes change isn't as hard as we make it out to be."

Freya's heart twisted in her chest. Apparently her words had sunk in, and that meant all the difference to her. She truly believed he deserved a second chance.

"I'm willing to listen," Cora replied. "Because I believe a similar friend convinced me that a future without someone to love is a bleak future, indeed."

Eldridge squeezed her tight to his side as the Summer Lord and Lady led the other elves down the beach. Their entourage trailed along behind them, farther than the others but still close enough. The elves with the Summer Lord all jumped from their boats into the ocean, then raced down the beach to join the handmaidens.

Now that she was looking at them, there weren't as many elves as she had thought. The boats were small, so they couldn't fit so many people without the entire thing sinking. The Summer Lord had brought roughly fifty elves with him. Only a small fraction of the Summer Court.

She'd have to track down the handmaiden who'd said he brought everyone with him and scold her.

"Where are we going?" she asked. Sand slipped into her shoes and slid between her toes. Though the grit should have annoyed her, she didn't mind it so much. Not when the moon was lighting up the entire beach with a lovely silver glow, and the elves were already singing even though they hadn't reached their destination.

"We set up a small area for them to all enjoy each other's company." Eldridge twisted their fingers together again, linking them even closer if that was possible. "I thought it might be smart if they were all together. Even the other elves."

She wanted them to have a few moments alone, but he might be right. The Summer Lord and Lady weren't exactly friends. They had a lot of catching up to do, and two hundred years of heartbreak and disappointment was a lot to cover. They might have forgotten who the other was, and they needed those moments to grow and learn from each other.

"Probably a good idea," she muttered. "Are we going to watch them all night?"

Eldridge lifted his brows and bit his tongue before replying, "Do you think they're both mature enough to be left alone for a while?"

She wished she could say yes. But already she could see Cora's shoulders lifting to her ears. Leo took yet another step away from his intended bride. Freya sighed and shook her head. "No. No, I don't think they're ready for that just yet."

"Shall we go babysit the children, then?" He lifted her hand to his mouth and pressed a kiss to her knuckles. "All we have to do is get tonight over with. Then we can finally have an evening to ourselves again."

Yes, that's exactly what she wanted. A quiet evening by a fireplace with a bottle of wine and her Goblin King stretched out on a sheepskin beside her. That's it.

But she didn't have that yet. And she was damned frustrated.

She sighed and started toward Leo. Eldridge framed her other side, his eyes set on Cora. They had to fix this before the two of them ruined it again.

Maybe that was a sign that they didn't belong together. Freya knew there was no one keeping Eldridge and her together. They figured out their relationship on their own, even though it would be easier to have a go between.

Speaking of.

A little black and white body weaved through the throngs of elves to reach her side. Arrow was out of breath. But he had made it here when she needed him most. "At your service, Miss Freya."

"Where have you been?"

He nodded toward the handmaidens, baring his teeth in a nasty snarl. "I don't trust any of these elves. I've been keeping an eye on the servants to make sure no one decides to poison the food."

Freya dropped onto a knee and patted his head gently. "We don't deserve you, Arrow. You're a faithful companion that no one could ever beat."

Arrow straightened his shoulders, sitting regally in the sand. "It's my pleasure. How might I help?"

Pointedly staring at the couple awkwardly lingering beside a table of golden refreshments, she sighed. "These two are bound and determined to make this meeting as awkward as possible. And Eldridge made certain that meeting was public."

"Why would he do that?"

She turned that stare to him. "Why do you think?"

"Right." Arrow sighed and snapped his jaws at the Goblin King who passed by them. "Ridiculous man. He seems to think his way of wooing is the only way to romance, and he knows much better than that."

"Apparently not." She stood and started toward the Summer Lord, knowing that Arrow would follow her. "Let's not interrupt at first. We should listen and see how they're doing. Maybe they'll surprise us."

And considering they were next to the refreshments, she didn't have to worry about looking suspicious. She did want a drink to soothe her parched throat. The sand was dry this evening.

Leo's voice was easy to hear, even over other conversations and the faint sound of musical instruments being tested for tuning. "I'm just saying, I think it's fine for you to stay on the island if that's what you want. I have a life on the mainland. You have a life here. It's okay if you don't want to return."

The look she shared with Arrow was one of complete and utter disappointment. What was the Summer Lord doing now?

She turned around and bumped into Leo's back, almost spilling her drink all over him. "Oh! Leo, I'm so sorry."

He spun in surprise, then softened when he saw her. Leo caught the drink in her grip and helped her still the wildly swinging liquid. "Please, don't apologize, Freya. There are many people here and anyone might bump into someone else."

Freya caught his hand and tugged him close so she could hiss in his ear, "What are you trying to do? Scare her off?"

"I'm trying to tell her that whatever speed she is comfortable with is how fast we'll go," he whispered back. "Was it not coming off like that?"

"No. It was coming off like you wanted her to stay here."

"But I don't!"

Freya pulled away with a bright grin on her face, even though she was grinding her teeth. "Thank you so much, Leo. I'm so sorry again. I'll leave you two alone now. Be nice!"

She realized her voice was far too high pitched for anyone to believe she meant what she said. But how else was she supposed to get her point across other than with waggling eyebrows and overly emphasized words?

The foolish man was going to run this woman off because he didn't remember how to be kind to someone other than himself. Maybe she should have asked Eldridge to talk with Leo as well. Cora's predicament was rare, and she imagined it was difficult for anyone to put themselves in her shoes. Leo needed to know how Cora was feeling. Really feeling.

God, she hated admitting Eldridge was right.

Freya picked a place far enough away from the other elves that they wouldn't bother her while she sneakily watched the couple in the distance. Arrow sat down on her foot and surveyed with her. "How bad was it?"

"Bad." She sipped her drink, then winced. "And this liquid is awful. What even is this?"

"Probably a honey wine that the fae make. Humans find it very sweet. Is it?" He reached for the cup and then took his own sip. "Yes, this is the good stuff. Eldridge wanted to impress Leo, apparently."

"Good?" She looked back at the crystal glass and frowned. "It's awful. I don't know how you all drink this."

"Well, it's not for humans, is it?" Arrow grabbed the cup from her and drank again, grumbling about mortals that didn't know what tasted good and what didn't.

For a little while, it seemed like Leo and Cora were enjoying themselves. They laughed together and meandered from the crowd. They sat down under a pagoda that Eldridge and the handmaidens had built, with twinkling crystal lights and white fabric that billowed in the warm summer breeze. Cora even scooted closer to Leo for a few seconds, their fingers nearly touching on the bench.

Freya was comfortable enough to wander through the crowd and take her eyes off the couple. Another table had been set up a little farther away and laden with food. Freya's stomach grumbled, and she realized she hadn't eaten in quite some time.

She loaded a plate with bread, cheese, and honey. At least that would give her a reason to not talk with anyone. Even the elves wouldn't speak to someone stuffing their face with food.

But only a few bites in, something happened with the couple. She didn't know if one of them said words that were hurtful or what. Cora jumped up and stalked away from Leo, who stared after her with wide eyes.

"Damn it," she muttered. "What now?"

Eldridge appeared from the shadows behind her. "I'm on it."

"Good," Freya grumbled, leaning back against the table of food she'd commandeered. "It's your turn, anyway."

She waited until he was far enough away from them before flicking her gaze at Arrow. The goblin dog immediately trotted off to "help his king", when in reality he was spying for Freya. At least their connection was tighter than Eldridge and Arrow. She wanted to know everything the King said to Cora.

Arrow returned in no time, but Eldridge and Cora were still lost in the shadows somewhere.

"What happened?" Freya asked, setting down her plate of food. "Things looked like they were going so well."

"Apparently Cora thought she was getting too close to him and then she thought he must think she was a harlot or something ridiculous like that. Being that close to someone else after so long has been messing with her head." Arrow shrugged. "Eldridge has it under control. Surprisingly, the Goblin King has a lot of good advice for someone suffering from that."

Did he? That was surprising. He had never cared about touching her, even when they didn't know each other well enough for those touches to be warranted. She still vividly remembered him dressing her in this court the first time they were here, and how that had made her entire body tingle.

Cora returned, this time with darkened cheeks and a sheepish smile. She tucked a loose curl behind her ear, though it popped out again. Leo appeared to think that was quite captivating because he reached forward to tuck it himself. Obviously, that didn't work.

The couple shared a small smile and then returned to the dance floor where many of the elves were already dancing. They were swept into the sway of bodies, curling into each other as though no one else existed on the beach.

How lovely.

She pressed a hand to her chest and sighed at the romance of it all. They might not be in love with each other again, but they were on the right road to becoming head over heels just like they were when they were children.

A warm hand tucked into the curve of her waist. Eldridge tugged her closer to the comfortable haven of his arms and murmured in her ear, "I think they're on the right track enough for us to dance. What do you say, my love?"

"Yes," she replied, staring up into his handsome silver features and seeing the stars in his eyes. "I think we could manage."

He swung her into his arms and spun her through the crowd like she was lighter than a feather. He held her in his arms with utmost care. And Freya knew with every spin that she didn't have to fear or lead in any step. While she was in the Goblin King's arms, she was safe.

In return, his gaze warmed, and he stared down at her like he'd seen nothing so beautiful in his life. His hands flexed on her back and his lips curved into a warm smile. "Freya, there's something I've been meaning to talk to you about."

A hissed, "Hey!" interrupted them.

Freya glanced over her shoulder as Leo and Cora spun by them. Leo gave her a thumbs up with a wild grin.

She chuckled and shook her head, "Well, I'm glad they're

getting along. I thought we'd have to follow them around like two lost puppies tumbling over each other."

Eldridge sighed, but still managed a sharp smile. "They're adults. They will either figure it out now, or they won't. But I believe they have a good chance. Look at them! They haven't been happier since we arrived in the Summer Court."

He was right. Both of the Summer Court leaders wore smiles that were brighter than the sun. And when they snuck off the dance floor and down the beach with each other, Freya gave a long, relaxed sigh. "Finally. I think they'll be fine."

"I do too." Eldridge tugged her in the opposite direction. "Now, perhaps we can sneak a few moments together?"

That sounded like everything she'd been wanting for a long time. "Maybe for a little while."

As they strode away from the crowd, Freya gave Arrow a quick wink. He waved a paw and toddled off to the drink table once again. At least he'd enjoy himself while they stole a few moments together.

Now, she could only wonder what Eldridge wanted to talk to her about that was so important.

CHAPTER 24

The breeze shifted with them and tangled in the sweat at the base of her neck. Finally, Freya felt like she could breathe again.

Eldridge held her hand in his, tangled their fingers together and tugged her this way and that. Sometimes he tried to throw her off balance and she'd immediately bubble with laughter.

They didn't talk for a while. Instead, they enjoyed each other's company in silence under the stars. And what a lovely silence it was.

A thousand twinkling lights danced above them. The waves crashed on the shore, white foam lingering on the sandy beach that cushioned her toes. She'd so rarely been to the beach growing up. As an adult, she didn't have time to wander the sand like this. Let alone find someone handsome to walk with while the moon lit their path.

Eldridge lifted her hand and pressed a kiss to her palm. "It's been a long time since we had a few moments to ourselves."

"It really has." She danced away from a wave that got a little too close to her legs. It would have soaked the hem of her dress, and Freya wanted it to be preserved for a few moments longer. After all, this was a rare moment when she felt beautiful. "I've enjoyed being here, though. Sure, there's been some struggles and frustrating things that have happened, but I like it in the Summer Court."

"Everyone does," he said with a scoff. "That's why I spent my summers here as a boy."

She frowned, a question popping out of her lips before she could stop it. "I meant to ask. If you're from a certain court, how do you have seasons here? You keep saying you spent summers here, but there are no summers in the Autumn Court. Are there?"

Eldridge quirked a brow and the small smile on his face was one of complete and utter mischief. "I was wondering how long it would take for you to pick up on that. No, we don't necessarily have seasons. But we still like to pretend we do. I'd spend four months here every year, and then rotate to the next. The children of royals can choose to do so."

The children of royals.

She forgot that not only was he the Goblin King, but that he had been a noble his entire life. Sure, it wasn't the same as being the king of the all the faerie courts. But royal blood ran through his veins.

To her, he was just Eldridge. A rather unconventional and strange man who had found her at a time in her life when she needed someone to force change upon her. And he had. Even though she had fought him tooth and nail every single step of the way.

Biting her lip, she ruefully smiled. "Well, there's the answer to that, then."

"Freya." Eldridge tugged her to a stop, still holding her hand in his as if she were made of glass. "I know things between us have been strained since we came to the Summer Court. I thought we were getting along well, but then something happened while we were here. Care to explain what that was?"

Oh goodness, there were a hundred things she could tell him.

That she was jealous because he'd given Cora a lot of attention. But in contrast, she'd also given Leo more attention than he deserved. She supposed Eldridge could have gotten jealous about all that, but he hadn't. Likely because he trusted her more, and he was very secure in their relationship.

She'd also lied about finding her father. She should have told Eldridge the moment she found him in the trees and that the reason she wanted Leo and Cora together wasn't entirely to save the Summer Court.

Or perhaps that the trees had told her to do all this, and not that she had pieced together the entire story on her own without their help.

Maybe she should start with the fact that she was feeling insecure and then the rest could come out on its own?

Freya released her hold on his hand and ran her fingers through her soft curls. "Listen, there's so much that I need to tell you. I haven't been entirely truthful this whole time. I know that Leo and Cora getting together again is very important for this Summer Court, but I... I... I'm afraid that in doing so you'll be reminded just how much you love the faerie courts. And how little I compare to the beauty here and all around us."

His eyes grew wider with every word she said, and Eldridge seemed to fall apart right in front of her. His shoulders curved forward, softening in a movement that she hated to see but also loved. It was times like these when she knew he wouldn't berate her for her thoughts. Instead, he would listen to what had made her so uncomfortable.

"My darling," he muttered, reaching for her hands again so he could hold them in his own. "Is all of this because you saw Cora's beauty and you feared that I wouldn't want you anymore? Because you aren't a faerie?"

In the simplest way of saying it, yes. That was correct, even though she hadn't voiced the fear to herself. She worried that he was going to wake up someday and realize she wasn't the faerie partner he'd always seen for himself.

But this was too close to peeling open her many layers and

revealing the horrible wound in her heart. The wound that had always whispered she wasn't as good as others. The wound that made her aggressive and push people away so that she was safe from their love. Just in case they wanted to take that love away.

She recognized when she was doing it, but Freya had never stopped herself from shoving people out of important positions in her life. Esther was the only one she loved with her whole heart, even though sometimes she was controlling over her sister as well. Because Esther was family. She couldn't leave.

Until she did.

Sighing, Freya changed the subject to something even worse. Something that she knew would turn Eldridge's mind away from this conversation and to another. "I found my father," she blurted, deliberately ignoring the question he'd asked her. "I didn't tell you, and I feel awful for it. But the trees have been keeping him, healing him, in return for getting Leo to do the right thing and take control of the court."

Eldridge's eyes widened even farther, if that was possible. "Your father?"

"Yes. Nearly the very first day we were here. I didn't tell you because the timing didn't feel right, and he wasn't in his right mind, anyway. I thought you wouldn't let me go back to the forest if you knew a wild werewolf was being kept in a prison there. But he's better now. I spoke with him." She pressed a hand to her stomach that rolled with the truth. If she kept talking, it would keep spewing out of her.

She stopped talking. She stood silently in the sands, watching the many expressions play across Eldridge's face.

First disbelief. He couldn't understand how she'd kept all this from him, and she had known that would take a while for him to accept. Then frustration, likely because it would have made everything easier if he'd known this from the start. Freya winced to see betrayal on his face when that was the last thing she'd wanted him to feel.

But she'd known he would. Of course he would feel like she

was keeping him out of things. Hadn't that been why she'd been so angry at him and Arrow this entire trip? They made decisions without her. And here she was, making decisions without him.

Eldridge licked his lips and took a deep breath. "You should have told me he was here. I could have helped."

"I know," she replied. "I know you could have, but it didn't feel right. My gut screamed to wait. That you needed to do this without knowing where my father was. I don't know why."

A low growl rumbled through his throat, but he eventually shook his head and seemed to dismiss the conversation. "We'll talk about that later once we finish this quest for the forest and put the Summer Court to rights. After that, we will pull apart why you decided you had to do this all on your own. Again."

Well, she already knew the answer to that. Freya was a control freak and when things were out of her control, then she didn't know what to do. Her heart pounded in her chest and her mind raced at all the possible endings if she wasn't the person controlling every step of the way.

And if he loved her as he said he did, then Eldridge would have to get used to that.

Then she remembered the worst lie she'd been telling him this whole time. The lie that had broken her very soul every time she saw him.

The timing wasn't right. She shouldn't have even thought about it, but the stars were shining overhead and the moon glittered in the sky. And Eldridge looked so handsome standing there in the sands, ready to forgive her for the grievous mistakes she'd made.

"I love you," she whispered. The words ripped out of her soul and flew into the air like an arrow seeking its target. "I don't know why it's been so hard to say, but I do. Every part of me aches for your presence. I love you with every waking breath and with every sigh of sleep. I dream of you, and I can't imagine living in any other way than worshipping the very ground you walk on. It has plagued me that I haven't told you sooner, but then we were here and you were so focused on..."

"Cora." Eldridge stepped closer, tugging her close with their hands raised between them. Love burned in his gaze. "I have waited so long to hear you say those words."

"Sorry if they feel a little strange," she replied, looking down at their clasped hands and knowing she would never feel more loved than this moment. "I know it's been difficult for you to be in the Summer Court, and I haven't made it easier on you. But I do love you. I promise, from now until the day I die that I will say those words every single morning and every single night."

"I'll hold you to that." He leaned down, closer and closer to her lips. "You are the other half of my soul, Freya. My heart beats for you and you alone. I hope, in time, you will believe that."

"I do." Really, she did. She believed he loved her and that the world stopped spinning when he looked at her. "Should I say it again?"

Eldridge stole a kiss, his lips lingering on the corner of hers. "Yes."

"I love you," she whispered against his mouth.

He moved and pressed a chaste kiss to the other corner.

"I love you."

With a slow glide, he eased his mouth to hers and devoured her lips. Soft velvet and a tongue that tasted of sweet faerie wine turned her senses to madness. She couldn't think of anything but him. Her entire being shifted toward him, wanting more than anything to be one with him. The Goblin King. Her strange villain in a story that had turned him into a hero.

When she pulled away, Freya blinked up at him with heavy-lidded eyes. "I really do, though. I love you."

"I know you do." He kissed her forehead. "There's still something I need to talk to you about, though. Before we continue this conversation or get lost in each other's bodies. I need you to know something, to hear these words and think about them."

Her stomach clenched. Words that she had to think about

before they went any further? What could the Goblin King possibly have to say?

Before he could even speak, a scream rolled down the beach like a thunderstorm. The deep, echoing call was one of pain so biting that it would kill the person who cried out for help. A man's scream.

She released her hold on Eldridge and peered around him. All the elves had frozen, staring down the beach before a few of them screamed as well.

"Leo?" she asked, looking back at Eldridge.

"This can wait." Again, he kissed her forehead before turning with her hand in his. "Run."

Together they ran down the beach. She could only hope the Summer Lord was still alive when they arrived.

CHAPTER 25

Freya's feet pounded across the beach. The screams never stopped for the entire journey as they raced toward the sound that echoed in her ears.

Please don't let him die. She sent the prayer out into the realm and hoped that someone heard her. The forest must be listening. It was always listening and if she begged hard enough then maybe, just maybe, she could save him before all this went wrong.

They hadn't had enough time. The forest should have seen that he was doing better. That he was so close to taking control over all those things that had been thrust upon him at too young an age. And, if they just waited a few more days, then maybe Cora and Leo would have done the right thing. They would have fallen in love all over again.

Breathing hard, they rounded a corner of the cliffs and Freya nearly fell onto her face. Leo and Cora had indeed been enjoying each other's company, but that had all ended in pain.

He knelt in the sands with his hands pressed deep into the white chips of seashells. His head hung low and sweat already slicked his bare back. The vest that had covered him, the one covered in gold, lay on the ground next to him.

As she watched, his skin seemed to roll. Not as if he were curving his spine, but something inside him moved. Like snakes slithered under the thin layer of his skin.

Leo threw his head back and screamed again, though at least he didn't try to dig out the curse that affected him.

"What happened?" Freya gasped, racing to Cora's side.

The beautiful woman had tears streaking down her cheeks. Cora pressed her hands to her face and shook her head, eyes watering still. "I don't know. I don't know! We kissed and then he fell like this."

They'd kissed? If the situation had been different, Freya would have crowed in happiness. But that kiss had caused pain while they were all hoping that it would fix everything.

Tugging Cora into her arms, Freya pressed the other woman's face into her shoulder as Leo screamed again.

Eldridge walked toward his friend, hands outstretched. "What can I do? How can I help you, Leo?"

The Summer Lord was incapable of speech. He opened his mouth. No sound came out other than a horrible groan. It wasn't a good sign. Freya knew next to nothing about magic or the properties that clearly affected the Summer Lord, but she knew this wasn't good.

Eldridge dropped to his knees and lifted his hands. The strange language of magic spilled from his tongue, and dark shadows erupted from his fingers. They slithered across the sands and tangled around Leo's wrists like manacles.

Freya couldn't stand to look at his rolling skin any longer, so she pulled Cora toward the cliff where she sat the shivering elf down onto a rock. She knelt in front of Cora so the poor woman wouldn't have to look at the two men struggling to beat back the curse.

"Look at me," she said, snapping her fingers in front of Cora's face. "Don't look at them."

"But he's in pain." Another scream echoed across the sands,

and the Summer Lady flinched. "I should do something, shouldn't I? I was the one who hurt him."

"No, Cora. Listen to me. That is not your fault. You know what the curse is, and you've seen the effects on yourself as well as him. His pain has nothing to do with you and everything to do with the forest taking its price." She smoothed her hand down Cora's cheek and pinched her chin. "You look at me, and not them. Eldridge is a very powerful fae. If anyone can fix Leo, it's him."

"I don't know if he can." Cora's eyes were wide and brimming with sparkling tears. "What if we're too late? What if no one can save him?"

That was Freya's fear as well, but she would not entertain the thought. Not now when she knew how much pain Leo was in. The forest needed to give them a chance, and all it had done was try to stop them at every corner.

But nothing could ever be easy in the faerie courts, could it?

Taking a deep breath, she patted her hands on both Cora's knees and pushed herself back up. "I'll go check on them. You stay here and please, whatever you do, don't look."

The last thing Freya wanted was for this memory to be burned into Cora's mind for the rest of her days. She could never look at Leo again in the same way.

At least, if he survived.

She crossed the sands back to the two men. Long lines had split open down Leo's spine, like someone was whipping him. She sucked in a breath through her teeth and knelt beside them.

If she could have put her hand on him without causing even more pain, Freya would have. Clearly Leo needed someone in this moment. His handsome face was unrecognizable and twisted. She wanted to help heal him, but how?

"What's happening?" she asked. "What do we do?"

"Nothing." Eldridge lowered his hands and sighed. "We're too late. The forest is taking its price and nothing will stop it now that it's started."

No, that couldn't be right. They'd worked too hard and now the forest would what? Ruin this moment? They were closer now than they had ever been!

"We aren't too late. I refuse to accept that." Freya reached out then, taking the chance to hurt Leo and putting her hand on his shoulder. "You must know a way that can stop this. I know you think you deserve this, Leo, but how can we stop this?"

He met her gaze, and she saw all the blood vessels in his eyes had popped. Those beautiful green eyes were now ringed with red blood.

"We were too... late." He stuttered over the words, each one ground through his teeth as he fought to speak.

Freya pursed her lips and patted his shoulder. "You're wrong. I know you're wrong, and you're thinking that you deserve this. As your friend, I will not let you make this mistake. So you tell us how to fix this."

Soft footsteps approached them through the sands. Cora stood beside them, and a slight wind ruffled the curls that had escaped her carefully laid braids. "I think I might know how to help him, but none of you are going to like it."

Of course. Why hadn't Freya thought of asking Cora first? This was the woman who was meant to be the Summer Lady. And though she had been absent from the court for a very long time, all the secrets Leo wanted to hide were surely known by this lovely lady.

Freya whipped around, sand blasting from her movements and dirtying the hem of her dress. "Tell us. You know we'll do whatever it takes."

But a frown marred Cora's face. "The forest wants to take him back. It's disappointed that it has taken him this long when it already gave us all the opportunities we needed."

"Yes, we understand that part."

"The only thing I can think of that might stop this is bringing him to the forest." Cora wrung her hands and stared out to the sea. "But that would take a very long time to get back to the mainland. And worse, I don't think he'd make the journey."

Freya snapped her fingers. "But there's a portal that goes back to the mainland. That's what I came through."

"It only goes in one direction. The portal was meant to give the Summer Lord a way to come and visit me whenever he came to his senses." Cora's expression saddened, and she curled her shoulders inward. "I don't think he'll make the trip, Freya. The forest is plaguing him. All that movement underneath his skin? It's turning his blood to roots. Soon, he will attach himself to the nearest tree. Just like all those other faeries who ended up stuck in the forest."

Freya remembered them. How could she ever forget?

Those dead beings in the roots of the trees had reached for her every time she walked by them. And though she'd thought they were being punished by the trees, she wondered if they were the disappointments. The cast offs that the forest had thought might entertain, but then decided weren't worthy of so much attention.

She licked her lips and whispered, "The trees keep what they love, even after they are no longer useful."

Leo flung out his hand and latched onto Freya. His wide, bloodshot eyes tried to convey some fear that she didn't need him to voice. He didn't want to go to the forest. Leo feared staying there for the rest of time, alive but not. Dead, but not.

If he was going to suffer, then he wanted to be here. Out in the open where the forest couldn't reach him other than to kill him. Maybe that was the merciful thing to do. Maybe Freya should let him fall onto his stomach, roll him over, and then watch as a small grove of trees grew from his body.

She looked over to Eldridge and saw tears in the Goblin King's eyes. Even he didn't think they could save the Summer Lord. She knew that guilt would gnaw and bite. Though their relationship had dimmed in recent years, Leo was still important to Eldridge.

Faerie realms, he was important to Freya too. She'd struck up a friendship with this ridiculous, foolish man who would sacrifice so much because he feared the unknown.

Freya covered Leo's hand in her own, squeezing his fingers as they spasmed with yet another spike that rocked through his entire body. "You want me to let you die," she whispered. "You are fine with sinking into the sands and disappearing from this world."

Though his features were strained, Leo nodded.

She looked up at Cora. The Summer Lady pressed a hand to her mouth and barely caught a sob. She didn't need Cora to say anything to know what was going through the woman's head.

Cora was so sad that she had only had enough time to remember that she did love him. That the feeling in her chest wasn't something that she'd imagined or forced herself to feel, so she didn't forget what love was. Their lives were intertwined and now someone wanted to rip them apart again.

Freya should step away. She should let the Summer Lady have a few moments with the man she loved, alone with only the sea and the stars to share in their sadness.

But she couldn't do it.

Unlike the faeries with her, Freya wouldn't give up.

"No," she growled. "I won't let you die, Leo."

She planted her hands in the sand and poured all her rage into the white sand beach. She let the ancient being deep in the earth feed upon her emotions. It ripped from her lungs anger, rage, sadness, and fear. It pulled all emotion until she was little more than a husk. And when she had satisfied the gluttonous creature that had named itself "ocean", Freya told it to slow down time.

A mortal telling the sea to help them was a ridiculous request. Even Freya knew that. But she didn't have enough magic to do it herself.

The forest had taught her to ask. The very fabric of the world wanted to help if only the person in need knew how to ask. So that's what Freya did. She made the sea listen to her, and she begged it to give these lovers a chance. All of her concentration and energy went into this singular task that might have taken all but a heartbeat, yet felt like a lifetime of battling with her will alone.

The argument was always the same. That the Summer Lord and Lady took too long.

What were a few more heartbeats? A few more days when the sea was inevitable? The oceans would never die in this place. It would exist long past the ages of fae and man. The waves would see new people take over the earth. The water would still kiss the sand even when time itself had ended.

A few days.

A few weeks.

Such bartering tools were not waiting for the ocean. It was a small rest and when it finally woke, the Summer Lord and Lady would be ready to take their thrones and lead this court into a prosperous age.

The sea didn't agree with her. But the more she argued, the more it softened. Like dripping water on a stone over centuries of time.

It refused to lessen Leo's suffering, but it agreed to slow time. Just enough for them to get to the mainland, and then she could argue with the forest.

Freya opened her eyes again and could hear a soft chuckle in her mind. The conversation with the sea had been entirely in her head. There were no words, only emotions and an argument that played out as though she were watching someone else speak.

This time, the ocean finally said words. "I will enjoy hearing about your argument with the forest," it said. "You're a persuasive little thing for a mortal."

Whispering under her breath, Freya replied, "My father was a changeling. I know the ways of the fae."

"You do." The sea chuckled again. "But not because of your father. You've taken on many of the Goblin King's qualities, but you have more hope than he does. It is a good thing, Freya of Woolwich, Queen Killer, and Lover of the Goblin King. Welcome to the faerie realms."

She blinked and the presence of the ocean was gone. Time had slowed, just as the sea had promised. The waves moved at a snail's pace now, and that would give them the chance they needed.

"Come on," she said, darting up from the sands. "Eldridge, pick him up. We don't have long."

The Goblin King stared up at her with wide, horrified eyes. "What did you do?"

"I begged for time," she muttered. "And we have little of it. Let's go."

CHAPTER 26

E ldridge hauled Leo to his feet, though the Summer
Lord groaned like the hounds of hell gnawed on his
bones. And perhaps that's what it felt like. Freya didn't
have time to pity him.

She raced ahead of them with Cora on her heels. Freya tossed
words into the wind and hoped the other woman would hear
them. "We need a boat. A fast one that will fly through the
waves."

"I have a better one than he does." Cora's brows were drawn
down in concentration. "The Summer Lady is always gifted a
boat that has wings across the waters. The ocean will let us use
that one."

Freya wasn't so confident. She had just spent a lifetime
arguing with the sea, and maybe the great being would rather not
help them any more.

With a flourish, Cora raced into the waves and raised her
arms above her head. Sparkling gold cascaded from her fingertips and sank into the slow swells. The glitter spread over the
surface of the water, reaching out into the sea where it disappeared into the depths.

Long heartbeats passed and Freya held her breath. Please let the sea help them this one last time. All she wanted was the chance to get Leo into the forest. The chance to get her father back.

A longship rose from the depths of the ocean. Its hull was solid gold, and though it shouldn't float, it did. The sides were carved with swans, their wings outstretched and their necks creating a bannister on the edges. This was a beautiful craft that Freya could only hope would get them to the mainland faster.

Cora looked over her shoulder with a grin. "Will this do?"

The sparkling lights of her magic still surrounded the boat. Freya thought the entire thing looked like it had emerged from a dream. All she could stutter was, "Yes. That will do."

They still needed to load Leo onto the boat and then get to the mainland, however. And though she'd argued well, and the sea was happy to give them the time they needed, she didn't think that included stopping the sea monsters from their hunt.

Nothing was ever that easy in the faerie realms. Never.

Freya turned and watched as Eldridge dragged Leo down the beach. The Summer Lord was slowing with every step. When he reached their side, she could see moss had grown on his shoulders and reached for his neck.

"Not yet," she snarled. Freya plucked it from his skin and tossed the moss into the sea. "I still have words to say to you, forest. I'm coming and you will not take him before we meet again."

Eldridge lifted his brow as she met his gaze.

"What?" Freya asked.

"You're impressive, that's all. I wasn't aware you were so... so..." He shrugged. "Feral."

She pondered the word, rolling it over in her mind before nodding sharply. "I like it. Feral suits me well."

"Indeed."

The burning edge of his gaze was one of pure passion. Though they didn't have time to entertain such thoughts, Freya was pleased to see she could still tempt him even when the world was falling down around their ears.

Eldridge's lips spread in a wide smile. "Let's get him in the boat, and then we'll argue with the forest as you seem so dead set that we need to do."

"We do," she grumbled, though she wasn't looking forward to it.

It took all three of them to load Leo into the boat. He couldn't help at all. His arms flopped at his sides and his legs refused to hold his weight. Freya grunted, shoved his legs over the edge and winced when he struck the bottom of the metal boat hard.

"Step two, complete," she muttered.

Eldridge helped her get into the boat. Cora leapt in gracefully and with no assistance. All the damn fae moved like water flowing through the world, while Freya was the awkward mortal that couldn't manage without their help. Eldridge vaulted over the edge and took a seat at the helm.

"So," he said, clearing his throat. "We're off. Just how many monsters are going to try to stop us this time?"

Hopefully none. Although Freya knew that was wishful thinking. There were going to be a thousand monsters rising out of the depths with gnashing teeth, ready to tear this boat apart if they were given the chance. The sea wouldn't make it that easy for them.

Cora leaned over the side of the boat and stuck her hand in the water. Her brows furrowed in concentration before she leaned back and flicked water from her fingers with the grace of a dancer. "Many. I didn't even know some of them existed. The sea will make this a battle and I fear we will need your magic, Eldridge. Otherwise, this ship will sink."

Right. This was Freya's nightmare.

Loud barking echoed across the sands, and Freya turned at the last second to see a black and white body dashing toward them. "Don't you leave without me! Don't even think about it!"

Arrow darted toward the water and leaped. His body arched gracefully, but then landed in a smacking belly-flop that looked horribly painful. Still, he swam through the water to the side of the boat where he scrabbled with his claws to get in.

She should have known he wouldn't let them leave without him. Freya reached into the water and scooped him into the boat. "This isn't going to be an easy journey, my friend. We're about to battle sea monsters and we can't have you getting sick."

"I'm stronger than I look," he snarled, although he already appeared to be woozy. "I will muster my strength for this. My place is with you."

Eldridge forced Freya to sit at the back of the boat. "You'll have to steer, Freya. I need to be at the bow so I can use whatever magic might stop them. Arrow, you sit with Freya and let nothing touch her."

The goblin dog straightened with pride. He puffed out his chest and took a very prominent seat directly in front of Freya. His legs were spread wide, ready to battle whenever the time came.

She didn't think he'd do much against the sea monsters. They would probably look at him and chuckle in the way only sea creatures could. Then they would chomp him in half and dive for Freya next. But it's still nice to know she had someone who would at least try to save her.

Eldridge gave her a sharp nod, and they were ready to fly across the waves. Freya hoped the sea monsters were also slowed by time, but that wasn't likely. The sea had given them one boon. It wouldn't give them another.

She steered them toward the mainland and into the storm clouds overhead. Thunder rumbled, but no rain fell on them. Almost as though the sea wanted them to see they were being hunted. And they were.

The waves were taller than ten feet high. The white foam at their crests bubbled like a witch's cauldron. Freya took them over the first dark swell and lightning struck nearby. The flashing light blinded her for a moment. When she opened her eyes again, the entire sea had come alive with sharp teeth.

A shark swam directly next to them and hit the boat with its tail. They rocked dangerously to the side. Freya made the mistake of staring into the water and made eye contact with a beast that looked like a squid. But its eyes were larger than her head, and its tentacles were tipped with sharp barbs.

"Freya!" Eldridge shouted. "Turn the boat!"

She threw her weight in the opposite direction and turned the rudder with a wild jerk. They narrowly missed a giant whale with teeth as sharp as a shark. It blew air from the top of its head and sharp shards of ice rained down from above.

Eldridge threw his arm around the swan figurehead, holding on for dear life as he spun his first spell. Shadows gathered around him, yanked from the very sea itself before he unleashed his magic. Each of the shadows took on a life of its own. They sank into the waves and darted toward creatures where they wrapped around each one like chains.

For a brief moment, the sea was quelled.

Then they heard a deep rumble. A scream that echoed and something massive rose from the deep. Freya swallowed hard and stared wide eyed at the giant wave that rolled toward them. Lightning flashed again. The entire wave illuminated, revealing the silhouette of tentacles as large as a ship, each one reaching for their tiny boat.

"Turn!" Eldridge shouted. "Freya, turn!"

Where was she supposed to go? There was no where for the boat to turn. Those tentacles were everywhere. The beast was larger than anything she'd seen before. Larger than a city.

She couldn't turn the boat because then they would head right into the mouth of the beast. Craning her neck to look behind them, she stared in horror at the rest of the creature's body that had risen from the waves.

It was a monster from the ancient stories. A creature made of nightmares and sea barnacles. The mouth opened wide, jaws filled with a hundred rows of teeth. She didn't know where its eyes were, or if it even had eyes. But the creature would not stop until they were in its belly.

"Freya!" Eldridge shouted again.

What did he want her to do? If they hit those tentacles, then the creature would devour them whole. It would drag them toward its mouth, and then they would never get out of its clutches.

Unless she slipped between the tentacles. And the only way to do that was to sneak up that wave and be quick.

Their boat was the fastest in the Summer Court. She narrowed her eyes and drew down her brows in concentration. Perhaps it was her imagination, but it seemed like the golden swans did the same. "Everyone hang on!" she shouted.

Cora dove for the bottom of the boat and wrapped herself around Leo. Eldridge sat down hard and hung onto the sides, though he glared at her for taking such a risk. She already knew he was going to shout at her.

And why shouldn't he? She was jeopardizing all of their lives in doing this.

Freya directed the boat at the small gap where it seemed like the creature was missing a tentacle. She thought maybe she could sneak through. Maybe.

It was a ten percent chance they'd make it, but that was more than what would happen if she turned around.

Every muscle in Freya's body locked up tight, and she guided the boat up the wave. "Slowly," she muttered. "Take your time until the last second. Surprise the beast."

Arrow pressed his face against her knee and Freya touched her hand to his head. Grinding her teeth, she shot the boat diagonally across the wave. It moved with all the speed of a flying beast, and then the tentacles came out of the water.

Great, meaty appendages swung over their head. As if the creature was trying to terrify them into hesitating. But Freya refused to let it scare her, not when she had conquered so many beasts here in the faerie realms. No sea creature was worse than what she'd faced thus far.

There was the gap. The smallest gap and she couldn't move until the right moment. She blew out the breath she'd been holding slowly, letting it leak out between her lips so all the sound in the world disappeared other than the next great inhalation she sucked into her lungs.

"Now," she whispered.

The boat careened up, up, up the wave and the beast let out a scream that rocked the slow moving crests. She set her grip hard on the handle that guided the ship and closed her eyes.

Perhaps it made her a coward to not see what happened. But in that blissful moment of darkness, Freya watched all the memories she loved play behind her eyes.

Death had come for her many times, and Freya had slipped away from its cold clutches every single encounter. If a giant sea monster was what finally claimed her, then so be it. She would gladly accept that heroic death.

But that death did not come.

They darted between the tentacles and slid out into a calm sea. The storm disappeared behind them with the call of the ancient beast as it sank back into the depths.

The boat moved with grace and calm ease. No more waves rocked the gull. They skidded across a mirror-like surface of water so pure that she could see the bottom. Azure light glimmered in the depths, and only kind creatures watched them as they passed.

The time for death had ended. Freya took a deep breath of salty, warm air. They had made it.

None of them said a single word until the boat hit the shore of the mainland. The soft crunching of seashells seemed to break the spell of silence they all had upheld.

Arrow was the first to speak. He snuffled loudly and then declared with confidence, "I will never step foot on another boat in my life."

A chuckle burst from her lips and then once it had been released, she couldn't stop laughing. The other two faeries joined her. Their laughter rose into the air, and all the last remnants of tension and fear drained from Freya's body.

"You know," she said, still laughing with tears streaming down her cheeks, "I don't think I want to get on another ship any time soon."

"Neither do I," Eldridge replied. He leaned down and picked up Leo's limp body, throwing him over his shoulder. "Now, why don't we go convince a forest that this lump of flesh is worthy of being the Summer Lord?"

Of course, they still had work to do. Freya catapulted her body from the ship and splashed onto the sandy beach. "I think that's a grand idea. It's been a while since I've shouted at an ancient being."

CHAPTER 27

Their travels would have been easier if there was a portal, but Freya didn't need a portal. She knew where the forest was now. If it hadn't wanted to be easily found, then it shouldn't have brought her within its glen so many times. Freya could get there with her eyes closed.

"This way," she said.

They all ran toward the small hole in the cliff where she knew there was a gap. They might all be able to fit, although it would be difficult with Leo. She pointed and made a small, disappointed sound.

"That's how I got there last time. But with Leo being like he is..." She didn't see him waking anytime soon, nor capable of walking on his own.

Eldridge grunted. "I can get him through. If this is the only way, then that's the way we'll go. Lead, Freya. I will follow you."

To the ends of the earth. She knew that was the end of that statement. He'd follow her through whatever adventure she led him on because he knew she wouldn't lead him wrong. No matter what feat, the Goblin King had always known she would keep him safe.

And she knew he would give his life for her if that was what the journey needed. Though she'd never let him.

Freya nodded. "Come with me, then. Let's go to the trees."

It was a lot harder to squeeze through the tunnel of rock this time. Every breath pressed her chest against the stone. And when she looked back, it appeared to change and warp for each person. It was trying to make everyone feel claustrophobic. Such a deliberate magic could only be the trees trying to slow them down.

But Freya would not be slowed.

She moved through the crag with purpose and determination running through her veins. No one would stop her. She would continue without question because this was the right thing to do. Even if the trees disagreed.

Freya popped out on the other side of the stone with a wet sound, as though she were birthed into the forest. Freya fell onto her hands and knees, already bowing to the trees without realizing what she was doing.

She would have bowed on her own, if they'd given her the chance. But they didn't.

The forest had expelled them right in front of the ancient oak that stretched its roots deep into the ground. The dead man looked at her with a maniacal grin on his face. "So, Freya of Woolwich, you're determined to become a hero once again."

"Of course I am," she hissed. "Why would you rush him like this? Even you could see that love was blooming between them again, and instead, all you want to do is hurt them. This was not our deal."

"We never had a deal. You were supposed to help me, and then I would help you." The dead man yawned. "I grow weary of your games of matchmaking and love. I wanted it to go faster, and since it didn't, I'm ending this game."

Cora wiggled out from between the stones and then dropped into a low bow. Freya wasn't even sure the other woman had looked around herself, she'd just fallen into a bow knowing that the trees would be watching. Arrow came next, his pointed nose lowered to the ground while holding his ears flat against his skull.

How ridiculous. This forest was trying to renege on their deal, and that made it unworthy of anyone's honor.

The dead man's eyes flicked to Cora, then back to Freya as though the faerie wasn't all that impressive. "I'm disappointed in you, Freya. I thought you would understand our need to see something happen quickly. Instead, you're arguing that we need to have patience. To show virtue where there never has been."

Freya scoffed. "Virtue? Patience? You're an ancient being. A lifetime of a mortal is merely a breath for you. I'm not asking for patience. I'm asking you to wait a few heartbeats so they can fall back in love again and give you what you want."

A single eyebrow rose and an emerald beetle crawled out of the man's mouth. "I'm unimpressed. Your fervor for the fae is unfounded. Give up."

Eldridge slid out behind them and yanked Leo's limp body through the portal. They both flopped onto the mossy ground, too hard. Eldridge winced but crawled to her side while still dramatically holding himself in a low bow. "Great tree of the ancients. It's an honor to see you again."

"Goblin King." Tree branches over their head shook and leaves rained down on their shoulders. "The pleasure is all mine. But, as I was telling your mortal lover, you are far too late."

They couldn't be. Freya wouldn't allow that to be the truth, because that meant her father was trapped here.

She had to save him. No other ending would satisfy her.

She straightened her shoulders and glared at the dead man. "You keep saying that we're too late, but I know that's a lie. We are here right when we were supposed to be. And I'm not going to take no for an answer, so you'd best change your words."

"Or what?" The dead man sat up, pushing his arms into the mossy bed and tilting his head to the side. Obviously the tree was intrigued.

Good. Let the tree be curious. Freya was going to sit here until the sun set on the world, if that's how long it took. "Give them a chance. That's all any of us are asking for. And all you asked for. You want them to be together, because you told me that was what you wanted. What changed?"

"Why are you fighting so hard?" He lifted a fist and opened it to reveal a tiny, glowing lightning bug. "Is it only for your father, or for some other reason?"

She wanted to argue that of course she wanted to help the Summer Court. At no point in this journey had her reasons been entirely selfish. Even when she saved her sister, it hadn't been just for her. And yet, she couldn't look away from the glowing light.

The light rose into the air and glittered like a mini sun that the tree had conjured up. She took a shambling step forward, lifting her arms with her fingers outstretched. Like she could somehow hold the light.

And she wanted to. What would it feel like to hold a tiny faerie in her hands? Would it make her like them? Ethereal and beautiful?

"Stop it!" Cora's voice cut through the magic of the orb. "Stop teasing her! We aren't monsters. We don't do that anymore."

Faintly, Freya heard the tree respond. "You think wisps no longer lead mortals to their doom? That kelpies no longer drown poor men who should never have tried to tame a beast? Do sirens no longer sing ships into rocks so their sailors won't fill the ocean with blood? Cora. You've been on that isle for too long."

The light was still so pretty. Freya's entire face and body were lax, comfortable finally and at ease. She couldn't remember the last time she'd been so relaxed. All her life she'd been tense, angry, looking for something that would make her feel strong when she wasn't. The orb pulsed and her attention focused on the light.

"You will not take her from me," a snarling voice echoed through the clearing and, in a blink, the light went out.

Dark shadows wrapped around it, holding on for dear life even as spears of brilliance broke through the magic. But the spell was broken at that moment. Freya spun away from the orb, shivering in the suddenly frigid air. Why was she so cold?

Blinking through the confusion, her vision cleared, and she saw Eldridge with his hands outstretched. His fingers had turned to black claws as he struggled to contain the ancient magic of a being far older than him. His expression twisted with rage and he shouted again, "To your father, Freya!"

She didn't need to be told twice. Freya dove for the prison of roots and branches. Even though it was made of the tree, she didn't think the tree itself could move. It relied on the dead things to be its voice and its armor.

Her father emerged from the shadows and caught her to his chest. "My girl," he whispered. "What have you done?"

All the faeries in the clearing gathered together. Eldridge still held his hands in front of him, muttering words that would turn into a spell at some point. Arrow stood on his back legs, ears still flat against his skull and his teeth bared, ready to bite. Cora stood with Leo's arm wrapped around her shoulder, and surprisingly the Summer Lord woke. Together, they weren't exactly the most intimidating of groups, but they were all together. Standing at the ready to take on a tree that she should have stopped.

Freya pressed her palms against her father's heart and swallowed hard. "I don't know. I thought bringing the family together might help them talk about their differences. It would force them to listen to each other."

"Or it will bring about the end of the Summer Court."

They looked at each other. Two mortals stuck in the quarrel between faeries and Freya realized she should have asked her father's opinion about all of this. He was a changeling. He'd been here far longer than she had, and he knew the fae like they were his own family.

"Did I make a mistake?" she whispered, eyes wide as she stared up at her father.

She felt like a little girl again. Freya needed her father to tell her everything was going to be alright. That she hadn't made that big of a mistake, and look, he'd fix it for her. Just like he used to do when she was a babe, and could still fit on his hip.

But she was an adult now, and running to her father to fix her mistakes wasn't an option.

"I don't know," he replied. "I suppose we should watch and see. But let's not look at any of those glowing lights anymore."

She had no intention of doing that again. The magic still lingered in her head, like the tree still had some control over her. Freya shuddered and stepped out of her father's embrace. She wrapped her hands around the bars made of roots and watched as her dearest friends fought an ancient power without her.

"You will take none of them," Eldridge called out. "You cannot force the Summer Lord to leave the throne. It was his by right."

"I gave it to him," the dead man snarled. "And if I want to take it away, then I will."

To her horror, the man shifted. He reached his arm underneath him and shoved with a bony movement that should have been impossible. The corpse lifted itself out of its permanent resting place and suddenly, it was a shambling, rotting mess of a person that stepped toward the group of faeries.

The dead could walk in this forest of nightmares. And they did.

Hundreds of bodies that had once been nestled in the roots of the trees stood. They all stretched out their arms for the faeries, muttering words that sounded similar to the language Eldridge used. A spell? What kind of spell could hundreds of elves cast at the same time? Considering they were using the power of the trees, Freya could only guess that such magic would be terrifying and powerful.

The Summer Lord shook his head, casting off the curse that

pained him. Or perhaps convincing himself that pain would not keep him out of this battle. Either way, he untangled himself from Cora's arms and took a shaky step forward.

"Stop," he called out, holding his hands out as if he alone could hold back the horde of dead. "It's me you want. I know that. You do as well. Take me and let the others leave."

The dead man who had been in the base of the biggest tree laughed. He still stood behind the others, either too rotten to walk or more interested in watching what was about to happen. "They came here of their own free will because they wanted to save you, Leo. I will not let them go! You did this and you will be placed in the roots of a tree where you can watch them slowly rot. I'll make sure you have a good view."

She couldn't just stand here and let them argue like this. Shouting from the relative safety of her prison, Freya pleaded, "You didn't give him enough time! This isn't about punishing him. This is about proving you were right!"

With a flippant gesture over his shoulder, the dead man ignored what she said.

Freya knew she was correct. The tree didn't want to be wrong, and in this instance, it was just as bad as the Summer Lord had been.

Leo took a step forward again, closer to the rotting corpses. "These are my friends and the woman I love. I will willingly give myself up to know that they are safe and alive after this is all said and done. I won't let you take them from me."

"You *will* all be together."

"That's not good enough." Leo took another step, so close that one lunge would have him in the clutches of the dead. "You wanted me, and now you have me. This is my deal, or I will fight with every last bit of my magic until I die. And then you won't get what you want after all."

All the dead seemed to hesitate. They looked over their shoulders at the larger tree, who was suddenly very upset. The man's face twisted in denial. "No. You can't do that. You won't."

"I will," Leo corrected. "If I don't have them, or if Cora is to suffer this fate as well, then this isn't a life worth living. I'm happy to take myself out of this game you so dearly love to play."

The dead man growled, but he looked to branches overhead and sighed. "Fine, then. If that's the deal you want, then that's the deal you shall get."

He snapped his fingers, and the dead moved to take Leo to his new prison. Freya couldn't watch the man she thought of as a friend suffer that fate. He'd given himself up for all of them. If that didn't prove he'd changed, then she didn't know what would.

A scream blasted and Freya turned in time to see Cora throw herself in front of Leo. She held her arms outstretched, face turned away from the dead.

Everything in the clearing stopped. Time held still. Even the motes of dust stopped spinning in the air.

Freya held her breath with everything else in the clearing. She stared at the lovely Cora, who intended to sacrifice her own life for the man she loved. Just as Leo had tried to do for her.

A great sigh echoed from the tree. And suddenly all the dead turned and shambled back to their places in the trees.

What was happening?

The dead man heaved another sigh and inclined his head. "Summer Lady, you were the one I was waiting for the longest. I see you've made up your mind."

"I will not let him die, if that's what you're asking." Cora straightened her shoulders and looked every inch like a lady of this court. "He doesn't deserve it."

"Neither do you." The dead man turned and staggered back to his own tree, where he laid down like the ancient being he was. "That's all we wanted. To know for certain that you and the Summer Lord were truthful with each other. A party on a beach means nothing. But being willing to give up your life for each other? That's a good sign."

Angry visions flashed in front of Freya's eyes. She wanted to take an axe to that ancient tree and force it to feel the same fear she and her companions had shared. This cruelty was uncalled for. Entirely.

The roots of the tree lifted and freed her and her father. They both took each other's hands and approached the waiting faeries.

Arrow walked over to her side and held out a paw. "Sir. I'm afraid I don't know what to call you."

Her father smiled and took the dog's offered paw. "Henry. You can call me Henry."

Arrow nodded. "Well then, Henry. Why don't we get you out of this prison and back into the sun?"

CHAPTER 28

T hey didn't leave for another week, even though Freya wanted her father home as soon as possible. But Eldridge reminded her that they needed to stay and help. Two court leaders needed guidance, and they were the only ones who could provide that direction.

Or, well, Eldridge was the only one who could provide that. And no one else could return home without him. Apparently.

Freya packed her last item into the trunk and sat down hard on it. The clothing within might be a little wrinkled when they got home, but she was returning with so much of it. The elves had made certain she had all the beautiful dresses she needed for giving them back their Summer Lady.

Not that Freya had wanted any of it. She'd go right back to wearing pants when they returned to the Goblin Court, though she appreciated their candor. At least they were kind enough to see what she'd done for their court.

The door to their room opened and Eldridge strode in. He held a pile of papers in his hands, then set them on her vanity with a heavy thud. "These all need to go with us, apparently. Is there room in your trunk?"

She looked underneath her, then back to him. "If I stand up, the trunk will open on its own. I can't latch it."

"They gave you that much, did they?" He shook his head with a wry grin. "Elves."

"They're very kind," she corrected, but then smiled as well. "But maybe a little overzealous in their gratitude with what we did. I don't think I need any of these dresses. They wouldn't take no for an answer."

"Rarely does any elf even know the word no." He glared at the papers and then shrugged. "They'll stay here, then. I don't need them, but Leo insisted I take them and look through all his accounts. Apparently he's not very confident as a capable leader."

"That's why he has Cora. I think she'll round out his weaknesses rather well." She hoped, at least. The both of them had a lot to learn about ruling an entire court.

But if Eldridge could do it with grace and poise, then so could the new leaders of the Summer Court.

She sighed and stood up, holding out her hands in case the lid to her trunk popped open again. The last time it had blasted open like something within had exploded. This time, thankfully, it stayed down.

"If we're lucky," she muttered, "We can escape before the clothing attacks again."

"Again?" Eldridge gave her a bewildered look.

"Yes, again. It's already tried to take over the room like it was spreading. I don't believe this is the same amount of clothing the elves gave me, and such a curse could be quite dangerous." She hoped her joke was landing, but of course, the Goblin King took everything rather seriously.

With a burst of movement, she grabbed his hand and ran from the room. He sprinted with her, concerned at first, but then laughing as they raced down the stairwell covered in flowers and sunlight. Freya wanted to sneak a quiet moment before they went back to the real world where they both had a lot of responsibilities.

For now, the sun was shining, and the beach waited for them.

She slowed down when they exited the castle, breathless with laughter. "I'm sorry, Eldridge. I didn't mean to scare you. I thought maybe we could enjoy a little sunlight before we left."

"How strange, I had the same thought." He placed her hand on his forearm and guided her down a stairwell to the garden that led to the beaches. "I believe this is the last task we have before we return to our actual lives."

"I suppose so." She tilted her head back and let the sun play over her features, eyes closed with the confidence that Eldridge would guide her around any obstacles. "Have you seen my father today?"

"I have." His arm shifted in her grip as he guided her around a fallen log in their path. "He's in good spirits, although a little nervous to see your mother."

"If I remember right, they had a love that burned hotter than the sun. I don't think he'll have any issues when he sees her again." She opened her eyes and blinked at the bright light. "Although, she might slap him the first time she sees him. She's quick to anger, but at least she'll be nice after that. He made her run around the entire faerie realm to save him, after all."

"Sounds familiar." He walked down a few stairs and paused at the bottom, just before the longer stairwell that led to the beach. "Arrow has taken good care of introducing your father to this realm again. He said it was the least he could do for you, so you don't have to worry about your father any longer."

Freya sighed. "I don't know what I'll do next. First, I was worried about Esther, then mother, then father. Who will I worry about now?"

The sunlight played in the dark strands of his hair. He looked so handsome standing a few steps down from her, with his finely pressed dark suit and silver skin that the sun had burnished.

Even his eyes seemed a little brighter. They twinkled with lights that never failed to capture her attention.

He reached out and tucked a strand of hair behind her ear. "You could worry about yourself for a while. After all, you've saved everyone you love."

Ah yes, she had told him that she loved him. The words danced between them, as if he feared she would try to take the statement back. But of course she wouldn't.

Freya wanted to shout the words to the high heavens and let no one take them from her again. She placed her hands on his shoulders and dipped low to press a kiss to his plush lips. "I do love you, Goblin King. With all my heart and soul."

"Good," he muttered against her mouth. "Because there's something I have been trying to talk with you about since before we left the Goblin Court, but things keep distracting us."

Her stomach tied into a knot. She'd been avoiding this conversation for so long because she was so afraid it would be something that tested her love for him. What could he possibly have to say to her that was so important? She didn't want to question her choices now, not when there was so much love in her chest that beat only for him.

Damn it. She'd been having such a good afternoon.

Freya supposed she owed him this, though. If the Goblin King thought there was something so important that he needed to tell her this now, then she had to listen. That was the way of things.

"All right," she replied with a shaky smile. "What is it then?"

He looked around them and a muscle jumped in his jaw. "Not here. I don't want anyone to hear this."

Right, because that eased her fears so well. She was going to fall apart at the seams. Hadn't he just said she could worry about herself for a while? What insane quest were they to go on now?

She didn't say any of that, though. Freya allowed him to guide her down the stairs to the sandy beach. She licked her lips and went over and over in her head how she would respond to something bad. That she would always love him, no matter what the cost might be. That he didn't need to worry about her leaving him in difficult times. Their love was strong enough to last through all that.

"Freya," Eldridge said with a chuckle. "You don't have to stare at your feet. I'm not leading you to your death."

Of course she was staring at her feet. She wasn't focused on where they were going. She was bracing for the moment he'd open his mouth and let out all the things she feared. "I'll keep staring where I want, thank you."

"Yes, but if you don't look up, then you won't see what's in front of us."

"Is that so important?"

Eldridge snorted. "I think you'd like to see it, yes."

Oh god, what had he sprung on her now?

Freya looked up at the beach and her heart stopped in her chest. Someone had opened a portal on the beach, that's the only way she could describe it. A giant circle of green grass filled with butterflies had appeared in the center of the white sand. Edges of magic fluttered like sparkling dust. Rose petals decorated the entire ground and floated through the air on a breeze that danced lazily with its prize.

She stepped up onto the grass, standing in the center of this magical summoning. A blue butterfly twisted in front of her face, then landed on her offered finger. Its wings were so clear, it looked as though they were made of crystal.

"This is beautiful," she whispered. "Eldridge, did you summon this?"

She couldn't imagine why. Freya turned around when he didn't answer, searching for her sweet Goblin King who had only wanted to make her day a little better. To remind her why they loved the Summer Court before they left.

Eldridge crouched behind her on one knee. In his hand, he held a tiny box made of a seashell. He offered it to her with a smile on his face so big, she wondered how it didn't split his cheeks.

"You kept running from me," he said. "I know this might not be the right time, but I fear no time will ever be right."

She let out a little shocked sound that sounded like a sob. Tears had already built in her eyes, which she dashed away because she wanted to remember every single detail of this moment. This perfect, wonderful, surprising moment that made her heart sing.

Eldridge opened the seashell to reveal a beautiful black ring. The twisted metal curved up to hold a dark orb that reflected a thousand colors wherever the sunlight struck it.

"I love you," he said. "From the very first moment I saw you, when you walked into my life like a storm. I knew that every day without you would be dull, colorless, and soul crushing. You reminded me how beautiful life could be, if I would only be courageous enough to leap into the unknown. You reminded me what it was like to not be the best at everything. But most of all, you showed me how my heart could glow in the darkness if I let someone be my light. Freya of Woolwich, Defeater of the Goblin King, Queen Killer, and all your other well-earned titles..."

He paused for a breath and Freya saw her entire life unfold before her. A life of happiness, love, and adventure.

"Yes," she blurted.

He lifted an unimpressed brow. "Let me say it first. That's how this works."

"Oh, sorry." Freya pressed a hand to her mouth and gestured with the other for him to continue.

"My love, my life, my Freya." Eldridge's lips twisted into a sideways smile. "Will you marry your Goblin King?"

"Yes!" she shouted again, then threw herself into his arms.

Eldridge caught her, tugging her against his heart and kissing her until she saw stars. And why wouldn't she? The man she loved, the one she would now marry, was made of galaxies and magic. She intended to spend the rest of her life loving him until she couldn't any longer.

Loud cheers interrupted their kiss. Freya broke away to see all the people in the Summer Court who had made her time here so dear and so wonderful.

Arrow shouted so loudly that people in the castle heard him, "Finally!"

Laughing, Eldridge released her to hold out his hand for Leo to shake. "Did you ever think we'd both get to this point in our lives?"

Leo shook his head, but pulled Eldridge in for an embrace. "No, my friend. I thought we would hate each other until we died, and then the both of us would die alone as old men."

She turned toward Cora, who was already reaching to hug Freya tight. "Congratulations, my dear. When Eldridge asked how he should do it, I told him something like this would make any woman fall madly in love with him. I hope it wasn't too much."

"It was perfect," Freya whispered. "Thank you for all your help."

Though guilt twisted in her stomach because she'd believed the other woman to be interested in Eldridge, too. She should have known better. Cora was too kind for that. Cora wasn't competition. She was a friend.

The last person on the beach stood apart from the others, but he was the only person Freya wanted to see. She walked away from the faeries to give her father a tight hug.

He sighed into her hair, then chuckled. "He asked for my permission this morning. I told him it was a little late to be asking, but that I'd come around to the idea of my daughter being married to a faerie. Besides, he seems like a good man."

Freya couldn't believe Eldridge had even asked her father's permission. He had been planning this for a very long time. "He is a good man," she repeated. "And I love him more than anyone I've ever met before."

"Good. That's how it should be." He kissed the top of her head, then pushed her away. "Go to your Goblin King, daughter of mine."

She didn't have to be told twice. Freya tucked herself underneath Eldridge's arm and listened to the faeries joke with each other. But it didn't take long for Eldridge to turn his attention only to her.

He kissed her again and whispered against her lips, "My Queen, let's go home."

CHAPTER 29

"**Y**ou're getting married?" Esther's shriek echoed through the halls.

The ear piercing sound crossed Freya's eyes, but she nodded before wiggling a finger in her ear. "Yes, I am getting married."

"Why didn't I hear about this sooner?" Esther shouted again.

"Because we just got home. My god, what have you been doing since we've been away?" She tried to change the subject so her sister couldn't ask even more ridiculous questions. She hadn't even seen their father get out of the carriage yet. And then what sound would she make?

Apparently another scream that bloodied Freya's ears. She walked away from her sister's meltdown as Esther saw their father. Of course it was difficult for Esther to see him. Freya had cried when she'd seen their dad as well.

But, as callous as it might seem, she wasn't as interested in her sister's reaction.

Her mother walked down the steps of the castle in a pale yellow gown that made her hair seem like golden silk. She floated down the steps, approaching her husband that she'd braved the faerie realms to find.

Her mother hadn't even realized that Henry had been watching over her. While her father had spent what felt like two hundred years watching over his wife, she hadn't realized a single day had passed.

Henry broke away from his daughter and stepped toward his wife as though she were a dream. "Is it really you?" he asked.

"I'm awake, Henry." Her voice caught on a sob. "I'm really awake."

Their hands shook as they reached for each other, and Freya had to look away when they embraced. There was clearly too much to be said between them, but neither of them was interested in speaking. They just wanted to hold each other after so long away from their loved one's arms.

The picture they painted on the steps to the goblin castle filled her heart with hope for the future. She could see herself in a similar situation as them, finally having her entire family together and maybe adding more.

If only she could paint this moment. To forever have it saved in some hallway where she could look at it when she was sad. To help ease whatever torment she might face later on.

Eldridge hooked an arm over her shoulders and tugged her tight into his arms. "How does it feel?"

"How does what feel?" She looked up at him and grinned, knowing exactly what he was talking about.

"To have your family all back together again," he replied, giving her a little shake. "Plus one, of course. We can't forget the most important person in your new family, after all."

"Lux?"

Freya burst out laughing as Eldridge swept her off the ground. He lifted her up toward the lingering sunlight and wiggled his fingers on her ribs. "I can take it back, you know!"

"Take what back? Spending the rest of your life with me?" She kicked her legs, forcing him to put her on the ground. "Oh no, Goblin King. You can't take that back. You're stuck with me until the day I die."

"Oh, I think that would be the perfect ending to this story. A love that will last for a thousand lifetimes." He kissed her, then smiled. "I could get used to living like this. You, me, your family."

A cold nose pressed against her palm. "And Arrow. Obviously."

She snorted as her goblin companion referred to himself in the third person. "Yes, and Arrow. Obviously."

Freya started toward the stairwell with her heart filled with light for the first time in ages. When had she last been so happy? Certainly not when she'd had so many responsibilities. Finally, she could relax and rest in her newfound life.

But the faerie realm had another plan for her.

The faint popping sound of magic came before she smelled it. Blood. The metallic scent filled her lungs, and she knew that her time in adventure wasn't over yet. She had too much to lose this time, though, and her stomach turned knowing she had a choice to make.

She could walk into the castle, away from all this, or she could turn around and face whatever had come for her now.

Freya had never been selfish. She wouldn't start now.

She turned with Eldridge and cast her eyes on the bloody scene. The stairs they had just climbed were covered in blood, like a red carpet had been rolled down them. And at the very bottom was a familiar, limp figure.

"Thief," she gasped before racing down the steps.

Freya nearly tripped twice before she landed onto her knees beside the Autumn Thief. Gently, she turned the woman over onto her back. Something had snapped one of her antlers off her head and the other was missing its tines. Blood coated her chin and throat, spilling from her mouth where a few teeth were missing.

"What happened?" Freya asked, hovering her hands over the Autumn Thief's body but unsure if she should touch the wounds.

"Death," the Autumn Thief gurgled. "Death came to the Autumn Court."

ABOUT THE AUTHOR

Emma Hamm is a small town girl on a blueberry field in Maine. She writes stories that remind her of home, of fairytales, and of myths and legends that make her mind wander.

She can be found by the fireplace with a cup of tea and her two Maine Coon cats dipping their paws into the water without her knowing.

Subscribe to my Newsletter for updates on new stories!
www.emmahamm.com

 facebook.com/EmmaHammAuthor
 twitter.com/EmmaHammAuthor
 instagram.com/emmahammauthor

THE STORY CONTINUES...

Continue the stunning finale of the Goblin King series in Of Fairytales and Magic!

Click Here to start Reading!